Best of

SINGAPORE
EROTICA

Best of

SINGAPORE
EROTICA

L.Q. Pan & Richard Lord (Editors)

monsoon

monsoonbooks

First published in 2006
by Monsoon Books Pte Ltd
52 Telok Blangah Road
#03–05 Telok Blangah House
Singapore 098829
www.monsoonbooks.com.sg

This third edition published in 2010.

ISBN: 978-981-05-5301-2

National Library Board, Singapore Cataloguing-in-Publication Data
Best of Singapore erotica / L.Q. Pan & Richard Lord, editors. – 3rd
ed. – Singapore : Monsoon Books, 2010.
p. cm.
ISBN-13 : 978-981-05-5301-2 (pbk.)

1. Erotic literature, Singaporean (English) I. Pan, L. Q. II. Lord,
Richard A. (Richard Alan)

PR9570.S52
S823.01083538 -- dc22   OCN609757104

Printed in Singapore
14 13 12 11 10   3 4 5 6 7 8

Contents

INTRODUCCIÓN

Introduction

Singapore erotica. *Singapore* erotica? To some ears that may sound pretty much like a classic oxymoron. Many, perhaps most, Singaporeans would themselves probably agree. This city-state and its denizens are known for efficiency, a strong work ethic, an obsession with cleanliness and a taste for law and order with fines attached. But high eroticism is something few would readily associate with Singapore. After all, citizens of this island finished next to last in a 2005 Durex survey of sexual activity (coming in just above Japan) and several of the more popular bedroom sports in other lands are still illegal here and occasionally prosecuted. (For instance, even fellatio can get you booked if it's not rendered as a mere prelude to straight genital sex.)

But as this volume attests, erotica is something of a boom industry in today's Singapore. Not only did the Lion City's first 'Sexpo' fair earlier this year draw huge crowds, but locals are increasingly finding their way to websites with heavy sexual content. Gerrie Lim's *Invisible Trade*, a seminal study of the high-end sex trade here, hovered at or near the top of local bestseller lists for months. And now this book.

Before we begin looking at Singapore's take on the subject, we should address the question of just what in fact constitutes erotica. One leading online dictionary defines it as "creative activity of no literary or artistic value other than to stimulate sexual desire." We disagree strongly, and we feel the selections included in this volume prove how erroneous such a definition is.

For the editors of this book, one thing that was clear—and that served as our guiding principle right from the start of this project—is that erotica and pornography are most definitely not synonymous even though they both focus on the same areas—sexuality and the human body.

Didier Bernardin, owner of the famous Crazy Horse Saloon (which opened a Singapore branch just last year) himself draws a sharp distinction between the two: "If there's more art and mind, then it's erotic; if there's no mind and no art, then it's pornography." According to that definition, all the pieces in this collection belong to the former as they show the keen creative mind artfully probing the contours and broad range of human sexuality and its various modes of expression.

In trawling through the many contributions we received, we sought only works that evidenced strong literary and artistic value. Of course, literary value has many facets, and the stories and poems here embrace various aspects, from the comic and ironic to the cynical, the wistful even the mystical. While some of our pieces address more serious issues, including some controversial matters that Singapore is grappling with today, others take a wry romantic tack or involve bittersweet reckonings with failed relationships.

Other than the quality of the writing, the one thing all these pieces have in common is their sensual—and often overtly sexual—content.

Appreciation and enjoyment of bodily pleasures is a very human quality and this book shows that Singaporeans can produce good writing which looks at sensual pleasures honestly, creatively and without flinching. Many of the pieces here treat the sensual aspects of the narrative with artistic discretion; others take a more head-on, graphic approach.

The stances on sexuality here are richly varied, as are the authors themselves. While most of the writers are Singaporeans, several are expats who have lived in the Lion City and soaked up its unique culture. Two of the leading figures of Singapore letters from the immediate post-Independence period, Kirpal Singh and Robert Yeo, offer the perspective of those from their generation, while at the other end of the age spectrum, writers such as O Thiam Chin, celebrity blogger Miss Izzy (Isabella Chen), Aaron Ang, Cyril Wong and Jonathan Lim explore some of the darker sides of sexuality or take up issues that were taboo until just recently in this former "nanny state of Asia".

Several of the stories here do not have any particularly Singapore flavour. For instance, except for a smattering of local references, *Self-Portrait With Three Monkeys*, *Celibation* and *The Phoenix Tattoos* could have taken place anywhere. For that matter, a quirky piece such as *Club Koyaanisquatsi* still could not actually take place here in the Lion City. (Visitors and locals can save themselves the trouble of trying to locate the actual

Club K. anywhere on these shores—at least not for a while.)

But most of the stories are "uniquely Singapore", reflecting the peculiarities and idiosyncrasies of this rapidly changing society. For instance, we encounter commercial sex as found in the local massage parlors or KTV lounges, sexual staples for many here. Sexual repression-cum-obsession, another feature of certain Singaporeans' sex lives, is given a sly treatment in *The Good Girl*, while prolonged virginity and its eventual welcomed demise is served up in a first-hand report in *A Dummy's Guide To Losing Your Virginity*.

On the socially acute side, the phenomenon and treatment of maids, especially the sensual and vivacious domestic workers who often flock here from neighbouring Southeast Asian countries, is examined from different perspectives in two of our stories.

Issues of sex and race are often deeply intertwined, and that is certainly the case in several of our stories (*Naked Screw*, *Clean Sex*, *Body Drafts* and *Night At Passion Touch* to name just four), reflecting the piquant multiracial, multicultural nature of Singapore society. At the darker end of the spectrum, sex as a form of retribution is given a chilling rendition in the flash fiction piece *Femme Fatale*. We also include a charming celebration of autoeroticism and voyeurism (Alison Lester's *Naked Screw*) and a sympathetic portrait of geriatric sexual fantasies and fulfilments.

To sum it all up, this first collection of Singapore erotic writings is a testament to the triumph of human sexuality and its potential for sparking off admirable literary works. It's also a testament to the abilities, intelligence and sensitivity of Singapore writers in engaging a central fact of human experience—our sexuality and the role it plays in making us who we are.

L.Q. Pan and Richard Lord
Singapore

The Good Girl

Alice Lee Am

"Do the summary on Page 58 and make sure you do not exceed the word limit."

She was glad for the twenty-minute break. She had been talking too much to a herd of dullards who did not bother with what she was saying and who were destined to fail their finals anyway.

She hated sweating in classrooms that were not air-conditioned, the hot and humid air serviced only by two ceiling fans, merely shifting hot air from place to place. Her foundation was streaking because of the humidity; now her pores would get clogged again and her acne worsen. She wished she had brought some facial blotters. Now she was worried about pimples that were sure to visit.

She did not mind teaching these people who did not bother to learn, but it was a joke to even call what she did teaching. She was just going through the motions, acting the role of teacher.

When she had just graduated from teacher training, getting the destined-for-failure classes seemed a humiliation. Now she was secretly elated when she got them. Nothing much was expected of these people, so little was expected of her as a teacher. She just had to follow the syllabus, mouth what she was expected to, submit a few reports and wait for her salary and bonuses.

How she despised these people who reeked of a nauseating blend of sweat and pimple cream. Many of the boys looked ridiculous with their hair assaulted with cheap gel. She hated those sluts who wore padded bras, who hemmed up their school skirts and wore discount make-up bought off some supermarket shelf. Make-up was banned in the school, but those tasteless bitches would wear their foundation and line their eyes with such care that it looked like smooth skin and smoky eyes were gifts of nature. "Cheap, ugly sluts," she thought.

But ... but Zul was different. His hair was never gelled. And he had an athlete's frame. He was all of eighteen years and looked a man, a real man. He could never be accused of being too brainy, though he was one of the rare ones who actually tried at his studies.

Suddenly she was reminded of what she was wearing. She thought herself rather clever: wearing clothes that were teacher-looking and seemingly decent, yet were meant to seed carnal thoughts of her in the minds of the teenage boys. It was a well-known fact that males of that age have one predominant occupation. And she was quite happy to add to their distraction.

Two of the boys were in fact staring at her chest. She pretended not to notice. She was wearing a white blouse that was two sizes too small. It was buttoned down in front. It looked like her breasts were fighting to get out. She knew there were gaps between the buttons where they could get a good view of her generous cleavage when she stood sideways.

She liked that blouse but it wasn't her favourite top. Her favourite would have to be the white V-necked T-shirt with the silk knit material. It was a miracle of design and tailoring. The tight-fitting tee added at least one bra size to an already formidable pair of tits. She felt like a double-D in it. But the best part about the T-shirt was that with a thin enough bra, one could see a faint trace of her nipples.

She felt a tingle between her legs as she thought about how when she wore the blouse the last time, Zul stared as she bent down right in front of him to check his grammar. She was sure he got an eyeful. He must surely have imagined squeezing and sucking her soft, large tits. He could probably imagine their taste, the feel of her flesh in his mouth. He must have been squirming. It must have been why he asked to go to the toilet soon after.

These people were not doing their work. Except for Zul and that pathetic Kok Meng, who had neither brains nor looks, no one else was working. Two boys were sleeping, three sluts whispering and giggling away, another reading a magazine, others walking around chatting, laughing like she was invisible. She did not bother. No sense getting herself riled. Stress was aging.

"Alright, you should have finished by now. I'd like you to hand in your books whether or not you have completed your work." She was sure she would get several blank page submissions. She didn't mind; those were the easiest to mark.

She was a little regretful the lesson had ended so quickly and that she would not be able to see Zul till third period the next day. Maybe she would wear that white V-neck tomorrow.

She walked out of the classroom with a bounce in her step that ensured that her breasts would jiggle. She was hoping Zul would notice.

She had to walk the jiggly-titty way. There was no other way to walk. She liked the stares she got from men, even old, ugly men. The stares had become part of her existence. She could not live without the dirty stares and dirty thoughts of strange men.

She had had an anxious few years, starting when she was eleven, wondering how big her breasts would be. It was perhaps instinctive, perhaps the result of what she saw on TV and in magazines that she thought "big breasts good, small breasts bad". She rejoiced when, at fifteen, it seemed almost overnight that she had an enviable pair of cup Cs. These twin blessings were especially welcome since she did not have a face or figure that boys and men would waste a second look on. Her face was plain, even a little ugly, with coarse features and angry red pimples and her body terminally plump; in a society whose men silently or not so silently condemned the unbeautiful. But with the new addition to her body, boys and men looked. They stared, to be precise. She felt wanted and powerful.

She did her first jiggle at fifteen years of age. It was a magnificent feeling. Just by walking with a certain bounce in her step, she could feel desired, though she knew little of sex then. Some girls in her convent school talked about it. She learnt little amidst the giggling and whispering. And she had to display, at appropriate moments, looks of revulsion, and mouth exclamations of disgust. But she knew sex was exciting. It was exciting looking at boys, talking about them and hearing about them.

Jaclyn Wong, one of the prettiest girls in school—slim and busty with long hair, smooth, fair skin and large eyes—even bragged about taking the pill. Jaclyn was the one who brought to school the magazine with the naked and half-dressed white women and the men doing things to their breasts and vaginas.

There was one picture of a blonde-haired woman wearing only a tiny pair of denim shorts who had impossibly large breasts, adorned with pink and pointy nipples. She was flanked by two men, one black and one white. The black man was squeezing one breast and seemingly sucking on it. The white man had taken the nipple of the other breast between his fingers. The woman's eyes were half-closed and her tongue was extended, apparently licking her lips.

In another picture, a dark-haired woman was shown wearing red panties, a red bra and a pair of red stilettos. One bra cup was pulled down and one melon-shaped breast accentuated by a dark, hard nipple was exposed. Her legs were spread wide and a man had his fingers in her panties.

The images in the magazine excited her and stayed with her. She wanted to be fondled too—and abused, treated like a whore. But like any self-respecting silicon-filled actress who denied having implants, her instinct was to deny. She had to say, "Eee, gross!" She was, after all, a good girl.

The pictures in the magazine inspired her to jiggle even more energetically. She was sure men who saw her large jiggly breasts were enthralled and wanted to ravish her. And each jiggle of her tits gave her a super tiny orgasm. She discovered entire days of nano-orgasms.

The day after she saw the pictures in Jaclyn's magazine, she was walking her usual jiggly-titty way when she passed by a group of three off-duty soldiers. They weren't wearing their uniforms, but she knew they were National Servicemen. She could tell they were conscripts from their age, their shaven heads and deep tans. They were idling in an almost empty coffee shop as she walked past. She had noticed them first and had resolved to walk past them with her finest jiggle. They noticed her and made lewd kissy sounds.

"Little missy, your titties are real big. Let me squeeze and kiss them," one shouted in crude Hokkien dialect to roaring laughter from his comrades. She shot them a look of disgust but was secretly happy that they had noticed and coveted her breasts.

That evening, after homework, she locked herself in her bedroom. She took off her T-shirt and shorts and sat in front of the full-length mirror. She slipped one breast out of her bra. She got excited looking at the generous mound of pale yellow flesh and the hard, brown nipple. She began to massage it and finger her nipple and thought of the images in the magazine. She imagined the soldiers in the coffee shop doing to her what the men in the magazines did to those women. She was greedy. She imagined one sucking one breast, another fondling the other breast and the third with his fingers in her panties. At that point, she brought her hand down to the space between her legs. She had always thought it an evil thing to touch her vagina, but that day she did not care. Her vagina was wet with her teenage juice and she instinctively rubbed her clitoris and soon experienced the most delicious convulsions. She did it again and again that night.

As a teenager she loved PE, where she had the chance to innocently bounce those large breasts as she ran and jumped; imagining herself to be the model in her favorite shampoo advertisement, frolicking under the glorious Singapore sun. Mr Lim was a substitute teacher who was fresh out of university. The young Chinese man with the broad shoulders, close cropped hair and big, cheerful smile was the object of many schoolgirl crushes. He was a rare male teacher in the all-girl school. She knew of classmates who wrote him letters expressing their liking and admiration for him. "How cheap!" she thought.

She saved her thin cotton bras with their almost nonexistent support for Mr Lim's PE class and she wore them under a white PE T-shirt that was too tight for her and barely contained her large, round breasts. Her mother had bought her a bigger, looser T-shirt that she hid. She was pleased with the winning combination of tight shirt and thin bra. Her erect nipples stood out and she was sure Mr Lim would want to take her nipples in his mouth, one at a time, and slowly lick and suck them. How could any man not want her nipples?

After each PE lesson with Mr Lim, she knew her vagina and panties would be wet with the sticky liquid. And it would feel unbearable if she did not do the bad thing when she was in the shower room. She thought of Mr Lim. She thought of his brown, masculine fingers pulling aside her panties and the two fingers that he would force into her juicy hole. She imagined those same fingers pulling down her bra as she resisted and pleaded for him not to defile her. She thought of those masculine fingers fondling and squeezing her prized melons and the lips and tongue that would suck hungrily at her nipples, one erect nipple at a time. She did not have the luxury of time in her school shower room, but she didn't need too much time to get to the point where she would feel extremely pleasured, then tired.

Mr Lim was there for only five months and she was sad to see him go. PE was not the same after he left. She was sure he looked at her breasts, every chance he was able to sneak a look. She was sure she knew what he was thinking. She was sure he wanted to tear off her bra and play with her big bouncy breasts—and more. That Miss Ho, who replaced him, was ugly, stupid, an evil slave-driver to boot, and her fellow students were not bright enough to hate her, she thought.

She tried not to do that awful thing that gave her pleasure. It must be a bad thing to do. She contemplated her dilemma with fear and anguish. After all, she attended sermons regularly and took her religious studies seriously. She was a good girl and good girls simply do not do these things; good girls do not fondle their breasts, spread their naked legs wide open, touch themselves and imagine men fingering their vaginas, fondling their breasts and sucking their nipples. Her guilt devoured her. But she could not help herself and masturbated as often as she had free and private moments. It was such a dirty thing to do, she was too embarrassed to even pray for help for her affliction. But one day, it struck her that what she did was not bad. The temple of her body was clean and untouched by men. She was not like that cheap slut Jaclyn Wong who had actually been close to boys. She was pure, she would not be defiled by men; and it wasn't that she wished the men she thought of to do those bad things to her. Of course, she didn't wish it; but she knew, she knew in her heart of hearts that those wicked men wanted to do those bad things to her. She didn't wish it for she was good and pure but she could not help the wicked intentions of men. And she was at peace with herself and her faith again.

She walked into the staff-room pantry a little too late to avoid the awful, foul-mouthed Madam Teo. The older woman was the popular and talkative Chinese Language teacher she hated. Her motherly appearance was deceptive: she could always be relied upon for keen observations often crudely conveyed.

She could never forgive Madam Teo for telling the two new trainee teachers what she had thought of breasts that jiggle.

"Of course, on purpose one lah, big or small, where can *neh nehs* go up and down like that if you walk properly?" And the young girl teachers giggled shyly. She was just walking in to get her morning coffee when she caught that snatch of conversation. She was sure it was about her.

"How dare she accuse me of intentionally jiggling my breasts!" she thought. She was generally one to keep to herself, and so when she interrupted, it surprised the little party. "Actually, you all don't understand," she said, addressing the three teachers. "And I don't really blame you because your chests are, don't mind me saying, quite small. So shy to tell you, but since we're all women I don't mind. I try not to let them, you know, bounce, but mine so big, can't be helped. You have no idea the sort of problems I have. You think I like it when men stare at me when I walk? It's really horrible."

Madam Teo wasn't ready to back off, however. "Aiyoh Miss Ngiam, no lah. My niece ah, wah! Hers so big like Dolly Parton's, I think D or E cups. Never see hers bounce when she walks," said Madam Teo loudly, following her little rebuttal with a vigorous shaking of her motherly head.

At this point she was ready to battle the Chinese Language teacher. "But hers maybe hard, not soft like mine. You don't know my problem!" She had raised her voice, her breathing was now audible and the smile had left her face. The two young teachers looked on in embarrassed silence.

The older woman relented and said "Ya, maybe everyone different, lah."

She had detested Madam Teo since. She forced a smile, and returned a "Good morning" to Madam Teo. She then quickly got her coffee and went to her desk to mark. But she was one who could multi-task. She graded, dutifully provided helpful comments on scripts and thought of Zul.

She could not wait to get home but she had her younger sister's birthday dinner to attend. How troublesome. What's the big deal? She was turning thirty-one, not twenty-one. Her sister had always been the shameless one, liking men and going out with them. Bah! She should just spend her birthday with that husband of hers then. Why invite her and waste her time?

She could not wait to get home.

She was pure. She was good. She had never been touched by a man, never even been close to one.

But that evening, she couldn't wait to be taken by Zul, by the three soldiers, Mr Lim, the black man ...

Clean Sex

Ricky Low

"Hey, Jeff, what's the matter? Why don't you just get a maid in here, clean things up, lah. You can afford it now, man!"

Oh, please. Whenever my friends—or wannabe friends—have suggested this, I have just sighed deeply, raised my eyebrows in a cynical arch, and slipped into my above-it-all smirk—a look that says, "You so don't understand what it's all about." It's a look I picked up while studying at Stanford. They've really perfected that dismissive look over there. I can't claim that I've mastered it quite as well as they do it, but I'm not at all bad.

While studying over there, I also learned the importance of self-reliance. For example, no real guy lets someone else do stupid household chores for him. Even when you get married, you work out a system, you share those duties. That's what being a full, responsible adult in today's world means: sharing all those stupid things that just have to be done. Having a maid is clearly a symptom of some weak strands in your moral fibre, as I have always lectured my lazy friends back here.

I've never told them the full story of why I feel so uneasy about having a maid. Some of it is that I am still embarrassed that my first erotic episodes involved the maid my family had when I was a boy. But there's more to it than that.

Like all fairly comfortable Singapore families, my parents engaged a maid soon after I was born. Actually, they engaged a few maids, but it was the third one who stands out in my memory: Hazniya. She joined us when I was about nine. She was the most energetic of the maids and, if I remember correctly, the only one you could even charitably call attractive. Like the other two, she came from Indonesia, had an enticing coffee-with-light-cream complexion and truly captivating eyes. She also had a prodigious set of boobs, the kind that assured she would never need to worry about drowning.

I guess I was always attracted to Hazniya, though at first it was just that kind of little-boy, prepubescent crush. As innocent as a plate of overcooked oatmeal with pools of skim milk. The sex part didn't seep in until I was about twelve. As is also typical of many middle-class Singapore families, Hazniya was often assigned the task of bathing me. I mean, like standing over me while I did a cursory job of swabbing myself in the tub, then telling me to stand up while she finished the job, making sure that I got all the "hard-to-reach" places.

Hazniya had been doing this from time to time, starting from when she first joined us, but one evening, when I was twelve, it all changed, changed utterly. I had already started thinking how really stupid it was having a maid bathe me at my age and was being sort of deliberately peevish as I washed myself down in the tub. Then Haz asked me sweetly to stand up, she wanted to see how I was doing. I groaned and made a face, of course, but that was the deal.

As I stood up, Hazniya bent over. I'm sure there was no intent behind it, but on that day, she was wearing this very low-cut shirt and a bra which formed more of a suggestion than a support. As she started wiping my arms and my chest, I was fixated on those munificent breasts, now a glistening coffee-gold from the light sweat the bathroom heat had worked up. I wanted to lean over and take them in my hands, rub them, kiss them, lick them, see if they tasted like the toffee my uncle often brought me from Scotland—or maybe the coffee ice cream I loved. They were, after all, roughly the same colour as those two treats.

And then it happened, suddenly, without any prodding from me, I swear: I popped the first erection of my whole life. At least, the first one I can remember having. This was a shock to me, and I mean a terrifying shock. I didn't even know what it meant, except that it clearly had something to do with Hazniya, and her bathing me, and that it had made this strange transformation in tribute to her. I stood frozen for a few seconds, and it seemed to get even stiffer as she continued twirling soapy concentric circles across my chest with the washrag. Then she happened to glance down and notice my boner.

I was appalled, hollowed out with shame. I wanted to say something, come up with some excuse, but I suddenly went dumb. While I was still choking on some words to spit out into this frightening situation, Hazniya got there first. "Oh, my, my, what have we here? Our little man has suddenly become a really big man, hasn't he?" She then gave me that warm smile that had sparked my puppy love for her. But the whole situation had changed radically. I yearned to grab her, to squeeze those fantastic breasts against me, to rub my new-found power tool right up against them. I wanted her to take off all her clothes, right there, then join me in the tub. I wanted her.

Of course, I couldn't deal with this at all, being just a spoiled twelve-year-old kid. I mean, this was my maid, dammit, who just two minutes ago was bathing me like I was a little boy. So my lust was instantly converted into anger. I scooped up two handfuls of water from the tub and splashed them fiercely across her face and breasts. I wanted her to look shocked, then enraged, to slap me maybe. She did none of that. "Get out! Get out of here! Right now!" I screamed at the top of my high-pitched voice.

And she, damn her, maintained her usual good spirits—she just smiled and said, "Oh yes, let me get out; I think Jeffrey is big enough now to take care of himself. Oh yes, I see this clearly."

As she made her way out the door, I shouted a phrase I had learned the year before in school and was just waiting for the right opportunity to use in social discourse: "Fucking bitch!"

I underscored the bitterness of that curse by hurling the washrag at the door she had just closed behind her. I then sank back into the tub and started crying, crying like an eight-year-old. I looked down and saw that my cock had just about returned to its normal shape and size. I felt … saved. But just as soon as that happened, I started thinking of Hazniya and those gorgeous tits and the damn thing started stiffening on me again. "Hazniya, you bitch!" I shouted out into the ceiling, hurt and anger intertwined in my timbre. I then reached down under the soapy surface of the water and gingerly touched the thing. I gently rubbed it a few times, as if to console it, to say it wasn't its fault that it had caused me so much embarrassment. "You bitch, you bitch, you bitch," I whispered as I consoled myself a little more.

Luckily, my parents were out that evening, so they caught none of my little outburst. Hazniya and I said nothing about it the next morning, or ever again. We pretended like the whole thing had never really happened. Of course, I never again let her near the bathroom while I was bathing—or even combing my hair, for that matter. She stayed with us for another six months and then was suddenly gone. She disappeared one week when I was off visiting an aunt and uncle in Hong Kong.

When I asked what happened, my mother shook her head sadly and told me that Hazniya had to leave abruptly because of some family crisis back in Indonesia. A couple of years later, my Dad confided that they had dismissed her because she had "taken some things that didn't belong to her." And some time after that, a close family friend told me he'd heard the real reason was that Hazniya got caught having sex on the living room couch with some guy while my folks were supposedly away. But I've often asked myself whether our little episode in the bathtub had anything to do with that sudden departure.

Whatever it was, we never engaged another maid after Hazniya left us. Physically left us, I should say. Her memory stayed with me for the next few years. During the high-tide period of my masturbatory youth, I would invoke images of

33

Hazniya whenever I wanked off: those warm smiles, the bubbly laugher, the wonderful eyes, those fantastic tits. The fact that I had never really viewed those tits in their entirety only made them that much more fantastic in my wank-off reveries. Of course, the fact that she was a maid, a live-in servant meant to meet most of our daily needs, only exalted my fantasies about her. It would take me years to grow ashamed of those fantasies and the exploitative relationship that underscored them.

That shame happened when I was at university. Political correctness ruled supreme at my school, and it was especially dominant in the Sociology Department. From my professor, Kander, and those plodding leftist texts he foisted on us, I learned what an exploitative system was embodied in the whole maid-and-master nexus. This was especially true when the maids were plucked from nearby, "less-privileged" societies—as Hazniya had been. Of course, all my classmates and friends at the uni subscribed to this view one hundred per cent plus. So I never volunteered the fact that my own family had kept maids from the Third World when I was a kid. I only confessed it to my closest friends there at the uni, and then only as a sign of how much I had grown during my short time at Stanford.

When I returned to Singapore with my nice, crisp MBA tucked under my arm, I fancied myself a completely transformed person, one damn enlightened guy equally well versed in business and life in general. I was also vehemently committed to self-reliance by then. Anything I couldn't do for myself just wouldn't get done. Period.

Of course, an MBA from an elite American school guaranteed that I could just about waltz right into any high-paying job and find a stack of perqs to perk me up. Then, two months after I started working, I started looking for a place of my own.

The complex that I moved into, the Chateau de Luxus, was optimal in many ways. It was right across from a big bus terminal, about an eight-minute walk from an MRT station, another short walk from a huge shopping centre, and it was populated by swarms of attractive young women. Admittedly, some of them had husbands or kids in tow, but a lot of them seemed to be single. The problem was, most of these women seemed to be staunchly single.

Watching them go off to work in the morning, or come back in the evening, or head off on weekend activities was an exercise in slow torture. Here were these luscious babes, with expertly coiffed hair, long, exposed limbs, fall-on-your-knees figures, and yet they all bore a demeanour that screeched, "Keep your distance, dude!"

This was cold beauty in its purest, coldest form. I finally started thinking of them as just lovely works of art brought in to jack up the Chateau's property values. Actually embracing one, I thought, would be like fondling a priceless statue or scratching on a painting in some museum.

Fortunately, this permafrost demeanour was only common among the sleek, polished women of my own class, mainly Chinese Singaporeans like myself. There was one group of attractive young women at the Chateau who were anything but cold; in fact, these ladies grew warmer and warmer after a few casual meetings and then regularly greeted me with a giggly friendliness. And in contrast to the cold, stiff beauty of the career women, these girls exuded an earthy sensuality that filled the air when you passed by them. I'm talking here about the maids.

Not only did the maids always return my greetings, before long they would initiate them, even move into casual conversation when the situation allowed. Which usually meant when their employers were not around. With the employers there, they'd revert to shy, conspiratorial smiles.

And I have to admit, I found many of these maids cute, some of them very cute. More importantly, for my tastes anyway, they were alluring in a thoroughly unpretentious way. Unlike the Chateau's career ladies, these "domestic workers" were not shrewdly wrapped in the latest expensive fashions with a heavy measure of makeup fine-tuning their features. These maids were more down-to-earth—more real, to put it plainly. No makeup I could detect. And their standard uniform consisted of short pants which only made their way down the top third of their thighs topped by tight tee-shirts or breezy blouses. Simple, straight to the point. Which, in my view, made these ladies much more sensual and alluring than the pampered lovelies of my class and race. If the latter were cold works of art, the maids were rich folk art made flesh.

I always exchanged greetings with the various maids I ran across, and there were a lot to run across in my complex. I sometimes got the impression I might be the only one without one. At the beginning, I convinced myself that my socializing with the maids was a byproduct of my liberal education: I wasn't going to treat them as mere servants or act like they were invisible because they weren't off in active pursuit of the five Cs.

But after awhile, I realised that it was not just my democratic instincts at work. I was actually pretty interested, sexually, in some of them. Just seeing them approach, I started to get horny. And finally, I had to admit to myself what should have been obvious: some of the appeal sprang from the fact that several reminded me very much of Hasniya. In about the second month at my new home, I started to imagine the unthinkable: having a little sexual dalliance with some of the maids. Okay, I imagined it a lot; I spun it in my head several times a day.

Actually, it was one maid in particular that sparked my fantasies—Liana. Liana, what a great name, a sweet blend of Mediterranean mellow and sultry Sulawesi swing. She had—and you'll soon learn that I had sufficient opportunity to observe— these lovely dark eyes, accentuated by thick, sensual brows. Her lips were full, dreamy, moist, with a pronounced tendency to spill into a smile. Her breasts were ... well, I'll get to that part later. Suffice it to say she had a fucktastic compact figure that cried out for closer inspection. Except that there was, of course, no chance to carry out this inspection anywhere in the common areas of our condo complex.

And this wasn't just a one-sided infatuation either. Liana had, right from the start, been the most forward of all the maids. She obviously had her eye on me. "I never see you with your wife, Sir. Does she spending all her time with the children? Or is it her job?" I told her I wasn't married. Her smile seemed to brighten up about 100 watts when she heard that. "Oh. Well then, Sir must have many girlfriends then. So handsome, and with that beautiful car." So, she'd noticed my wheels. Good, that's what they were there for, right? And while handsome might be stretching it a few categories, I am sort of cute ... in a subtle way.

"Well, no steady girlfriend at the moment. I'm sort of keeping my options open." This phrase seemed to puzzle her, so I swung back to straightforward. "No, I don't have any regular girlfriend at the moment. Still looking for the right lady." Again, that smile lit up like a fireworks display.

"Oh," she'd say, "I think Sir is just being modest."

Unfortunately, Sir was not being at all modest. While I had dated a number of women over the half year I'd been back, I hadn't had sex—well, you know, real live sex—since returning from the states. And six months without sex, that is not good for one's health or one's self-esteem. What good was all my independence really doing me? When I moved in, I thought it would be great: no sneaking a woman past Mom and Dad to get her to my bedroom. But not a single lovely had come anywhere near that waiting sanctuary.

However, Liana and I grew more and more friendly as the weeks went by. The challenge was how to get her back to my place. Fortunately, this was less of a problem than it would have been with many of the other maids. Unlike most of the domestics prowling the Chateau, Liana did not have any high-energy kids to look after. Or bathe, I reminded myself with relief. She took care of some frail old woman who apparently lived alone in the complex. Well, not really alone, of course, Liana was there with her most of the time.

Her actual employers, I came to learn, were the old woman's son and daughter-in-law. They had their own condo over in the East Annexe of the complex. They would drop by quickly in the evening to look in on Mom, and occasionally swing by on the weekends to take the old lady and Liana off for some excursion.

The son always had this loose, distracted look about him. When we'd run into each other and say hello, he'd flash an embarrassed smile that looked more like a wince. Then he'd shrug, like he wished he could have given more to that smile, but had lost it somewhere along the way.

The daughter-in-law was going to be my real hurdle, the way I saw it. She was this perpetually wound-up bitch, who eyed me suspiciously whenever I crossed her path. Okay, she probably eyed everyone she came across suspiciously, she was that type. But I personalised it, as I tend to do with these things. Behind it all, I suspected that she might just be very insightful and could somehow sense how much I wanted to get my hands on Mom's curvaceous caregiver.

But like I said, distracted Sonny and the Wicked Bitch of the East only dropped by for a quick peek each evening and were absent the rest of the time. That meant the only one between me and luscious Liana was the old lady. I didn't see her causing any problem either, because this particular auntie was apparently not terribly aware of what was going on around her. In fact, after a short time, Liana and I would flirt along the pathway or in the lift with the auntie right there, just staring out into space, evidently oblivious to my presence—or at least my intentions. Even better, the auntie tended to nod off for long periods during the day, which allowed Liana to slip out quickly and do personal errands or schmooze with her maid friends. Now I just needed the opportunity to make some arrangements with Liana herself.

Early one evening, we ran into each other at the shopping centre. "Is Sir buying something?" she asked, blithely ignoring the half-full shopping basket that I was lugging.

"Yah, I had to pick up a few things I need before the weekend." We happened to be standing near the checkout counter at that point. A blush tinged her dark cheeks as she glanced over at one of the displays there, then turned back quickly, her eyes cast down towards the floor.

"Sir will probably have to buy some packages of those things for his weekend, I think." I turned to see what she was referring to. The first thing I saw was what she must have seen: the condom display. A rather ample condom display actually. I was stunned, though clearly not in any unpleasant way. I just couldn't …

When I looked back at Liana, she had just peeked up at me, a delectably impish smile on her face. Wondering what the fuck to say, I stammered out "I … I think I have enough of those already." I swallowed deeply. The next thing I said could carry me to either bliss or disaster. I had to be very clever, very polished. "You going back to the Chateau right after this?"

Don't smirk; it was clever enough. Liana flashed another of her bountiful smiles and said she had to pay first, holding up two cans of sugar cane juice. I pointed out that paying would be advisable, then told her to put them in my basket and I'd pay for everything. We could settle up later, I added.

We then joined the queue, with Liana standing right behind me. It was like some guy shopping with his maid, I thought. Then I realised I wasn't at all unhappy with that. If anyone saw us, they'd never think I was about to hit on a maid from my complex. They'd think we were just ... hey, another maid and her well-heeled employer. But I suddenly decided I didn't care what they thought. What business did they have thinking about us anyway? To hell with them, right?

As we strolled back to the Chateau, I asked Liana if she had any boyfriends here in Singapore. She told me the guys here did not seem to like her. I told her I found that extremely hard to believe. She just smiled sweetly, as if she didn't believe it herself. I then asked if she had any boyfriends back in Sulawesi. She had a few, she told me, but they weren't serious. "Just a bunch of stupid boys," she said. "Stupid, stupid, stupid."

By this time, I was finding it a little hard to walk since I was grappling with an erection that was caught in my boxers, jutting out sideways. This was no big handicap, though, as Liana herself was not able to move too quickly in her tattered flip-flops. Thanks to these two restraints, the stroll back was long and leisurely. We laughed and giggled a lot, though I can't for the life of me remember what we were laughing about. As we waited for the green light just across from the Chateau, I decided to make my move. I asked her if she'd like to come down to my apartment sometime soon, maybe have some tea and cookies. She said she preferred the sugar cane juice. I told her I was friends with a major supplier. She asked when she should come. I asked when she could come.

We arranged for her to come over early Saturday afternoon. "Sir" and "Ma'am" were going off to visit friends in Malaysia this weekend, and she said she could drop in when her auntie had her naptime. "Great. Oh, we should spend some time together over at my place," I added.

"No problem," she promised. "My auntie usually takes a long nap in the middle of the day." I really liked the way she said "lo-ong." My cock somehow managed to stiffen even more as it found another nook at the side of my boxers to snuggle into. I could barely move. But for Liana and me, it just remained to work out the logistics.

She had told me that her auntie usually dozed off right after lunch. That should be about a quarter past one, she thought. But it was almost three by the time she finally arrived. I was going crazy by then, scanning some of the DVDs I'd pulled out to try to distract myself while waiting for her. But it was worth the wait. When she finally stood there in the doorway, she was just so hopelessly lovely. She had done something special with her hair and even put on a bit of lipstick. As much as I loved her natural look, she was even more alluring with this little touchup. I had a hard-on within seconds.

I offered her some sugar cane juice. She said she would love some. Then she shyly asked if I could add some alcohol to it.

"Sure," I answered, "no problem." I reached into the back of my cupboard for a bottle of vodka.

She scooped up the glass, then downed the whole thing in one long swallow. "Sorry," she said, "I was so thirsty."

"Nothing to apologise for," I replied, then asked if she wanted a refill.

She nodded, but added, "Just half a glass." While I was still pouring, she turned and glanced at the kitchen floor. "Oh," she sort of squeaked. "You really need your floor cleaned."

"Oh yeah, but it's alright," I replied. "I ... I always leave it until Sunday. I look forward to doing it right after morning coffee and the *Sunday Times.*"

I doubt she even heard me. She looked around quickly and then, as if guided by some preternatural instinct all Indonesian girls born to be maids have, headed for the cabinet under the sink where I keep what few cleanup items I have. She enthusiastically hauled out a rarely used bucket, a scrubbing brush, a couple of rags and some liquid that I guess you use to clean floors. She was amazing; I don't think I could have found those things so quickly.

"It's alright, it's alright," I said.

"Oh no, Sir, this floor really needs a good clean."

"Just leave it," I barked. "I'll ... I'll take care of it later so you can get a good sleep tonight. I promise."

Liana had moved to the kitchen sink and was running hot water into the bucket. "No, this is good, so. I really like cleaning floors. It's so much fun."

While I moped, she mopped. And then things got more

interesting. "I hope you don't mind, Sir. But it always gets so hot when I do this work." Before I could ask her what I was supposed to not mind, she had swiftly tugged off her tight-fitting tee and with one further, deft movement removed the bra as well. She stood there with those luscious coffee-toned breasts topped by dark nipples and a kid's-party smile spread all over her face. She looked down briefly, as if to check what had me so transfixed, then looked back up, her smile conveying a sense of total understanding and agreement. She then swivelled and flipped the bra and tee onto the kitchen table with all the grace and artfulness of a stripper.

Oh my God, she was a fucking work of art under that maid's attire. Her skin was soft, light brown, the shade of coffee just the way I love it. Probably just as sweet, too, I was thinking. Although Liana was of small stature, her tits were fantastic: not as large as I imagine Hazniya's were, but sizeable and perfectly sculpted. I wanted to clutch them in my palms and moved towards her with every intention of doing so.

Holy wake up, I couldn't stand it. I had such a massive hard-on, I thought it might choke me. I figured if I couldn't put it into her, and very soon, I'd probably start ramming myself against a wall until I collapsed from exhaustion and multiple abrasions.

But she seemed obsessed with getting that damn floor clean. Desperate to plunge myself into this lady, I moved to the very edge of the soapy circle and reached out for her. But she pushed me off. With a poised smile and a no-no shake of her head, she said, "Not yet, Sir Jeffrey. I have to start scrubbing first."

Then she said something else that made me crazy. "Oh,"

she said, "I wore my very special panties today, you know." She unhooked her shorts and opened them to show me the knickers: a splashy swirl of bright colours. They looked like they'd been designed by someone whose usual job was turning out ice kachang. "I always wear them for special days. But I don't want them to get wet. Would you mind it if I ...?"

I guess she took my tongue hanging down over my chin as the closest I could get to "No, I don't mind!" because within a few seconds she had pulled off both shorts and pants, then carried them over to the kitchen table too. And, wah, could she sashay that perfect little tush as she made the journey. As great as her tits were, I'm ready to concede the ass may have even topped it. I couldn't believe this was really happening to me. And then she turned around again, and I saw her pussy fully for the first time. Oh God. It was a beautiful crop of dark, wiry hair, as lovely, dark and deep as the Indonesian rain forest.

I felt like lunging over there, grabbing her and then carrying her off to the bedroom, like Tarzan bringing Jane to his boudoir in the trees. But I thought that might spook her, ruin the whole moment. No, I had to practice a little patience. At this point, however, my patience had an expected shelf life of about five seconds.

She was now down on her knees with a wet rag in her hand, but before she began scrubbing, she looked up and flashed me another quick smile. She then commenced with the cleaning. She swabbed the rag against the floor in small circles, her ass and tits rotating in syncopated rhythms to this entrancing motion. She seemed so concentrated as she applied delicate pressure to those circles she was making on the tiles.

I suddenly noticed that I was unconsciously making similar strokes with my right hand across my groin. I started to sputter out a plea—or maybe it was a confession of love. "Liana, I ... the thing is, why I really wanted you to come down here today ..."

She looked up to listen, then flashed the most knowing smile I'd ever seen and spun my life around. "Oh, this is such hard work. I don't think I can do it all myself. Don't you want to help me, Sir?"

"Help you? You mean ...?" Without dimming her smile one click, she nodded towards the floor, with its sodden field of white-capped mounds. I tore off my clothes as quickly as I could; I tossed them back into the other room with the rest of my stuff, then rushed over to Liana and the bucket, sliding along the last stretch of the slick surface on my knees.

She handed me a rag and together we started working on the tiles. After a few moments, I started gently rubbing the rag along her ass. She gave a soft purring sound at this. I started to move the rag up the small of her back, making small concentric circles as I moved. Meanwhile, she had started rubbing my chest with her rag, gently rotating it the way Hazniya did when I was a kid. She put the rag down and used her finger to wipe behind my ears. I was in high ecstasy.

But that was just the prelude. As my rag was making its way up around her shoulders, she put both her hands on mine. "Now we come to the best part of cleaning floors," she said. And then she gave me a gentle kiss, as sweet as any kiss I can remember.

She pushed her rag a short distance behind her, took the other rag from me, then retrieved the third from the soapy depths of the bucket. She turned and laid all three out along the floor. After making sure they were all set at the right distance and fluffed up properly, she laid down across them, like they were some makeshift bed. She raised her legs in V-shapes, then stretched out her arms and drew me down on top of her. As I was sliding a little on the wet tiles, I was a bit clumsy about getting in just the right position. But I managed to get more or less right while Liana stretched out her hand, stroked my cock gently, then guided me into herself.

I was so horny by now, I almost came within seconds of entering her. But Liana somehow arched her hips rather acrobatically, thrusting my cock into a new position that held off ejaculation. I looked down into her lovely face in surprise and admiration. Any thoughts I had had that she might be an innocent short on useful experience completely disappeared.

Her pussy felt fantastic, especially in the position she now had me wedged into. It was moist and warm and wonderfully tight, and we felt like a perfect fit together. If anything, I was the innocent here. I whispered that I thought this would be even better in the bedroom.

At this, she just giggled warmly. "But we have to get your floor cleaned first. This is how we get to all the hard-to-reach places." Aha! Those "hard-to-reach places." I wondered if that was a phrase they learned at Indonesian maid school.

I was also wondering if she knew what she was talking about when she started pushing with her feet, propelling both of us along the floor. We would glide along the slick, sudsy surface, twisting slightly, her pussy rubbing my cock deliciously, my cock deftly stroking her pussy. Although I was on top of her physically, she was clearly on top of the situation, directing our slippery voyage along the floor, or the rubbing together and thrusting of our respective pleasure packs.

After a short time, I discovered how I could direct our movements a little myself, using my knees to get short, thrusting jerks, then giving a push along the floor with my toes, sending us sliding along a few feet, still locked together.

A couple of times, she would say she'd missed a spot. And then she'd start sliding back, her hands and ass rowing us backwards. She would again start to move her luscious ass from side to side, then raise her hips slightly and swivel. I'd go crazy. So would she. She'd moan, "Oh yes, I think we got it this time, that hard-to-get spot," and then give out that little syncopated squeal of hers that I found such a turn-on. So I would answer, "Let me give it some thorough rubbing, to make sure we've really got it clean this time." And then I'd thrust myself down into her lovingly, again and again.

We moved all around the kitchen, shaking the table, knocking over a couple of chairs. A few times—yeah, I think it was three, but I like to believe it could have been four or five—Liana would suddenly sail us along a wall or into a corner. She'd be pinned there and suddenly thrust her hips back and forth energetically, reaching orgasm after about ten seconds. She'd clutch me by my neck, maybe pull my hair and moan in the most wonderful way, then slip into a mode of release with a deep smile. On the last corner stop, I joined in, my cock going at about five throbs a second, my semen flowing into her in full, rich jerks. We lay there on the floor for maybe another few minutes, wiped out and absolutely ecstatic. This, I realised, is what sex was supposed to be when they first came up with the idea.

After, like I say, a few minutes of still lying there locked together, Liana looked up at me with a slightly sad expression and said she had to hurry back upstairs to look after her auntie. I nodded just as sadly, and said I'd help her get ready.

Ironically after all that sloshing around in soap and water, we both needed to take a shower. Which we did together, of course. We also washed our hair, which was drenched in streams of detergent suds. Afterwards, as Liana dried her luscious body with a towel, I started to get at her hair with the hair dryer. When she finished with that great bod, she dropped the towel and took the hair dryer from me to finish the job. At one point, I took the dryer back from her, switched it to cool, and pointed it towards her pubic hair. After a few rounds with the dryer, I reached down, said, "Let me check that it's really dry there," and started stroking the bush. By this time, I myself was already as hard as a graphite rod, and I started to gently insert my middle finger up inside her. "The hair's fine," I noted, "but I think this is a little wet here." She nudged me back gently and tsked.

"Oh, Sir Jeffrey is very much horny today. But I have to get back to my auntie or I might get in really trouble. We'll be back to check on the floor in a few days, though."

For the next two months, my kitchen floor was kept stunningly clean. Liana and I would attend to it at least once a week, sometimes even two or three times, depending on how often she could sneak out of her place and down to mine. It sparkled, that floor. I never realised the happiness I could feel just having such a sparkling floor to look at.

Usually, we'd proceed the way we had the first time, but sometimes Liana would ask if she could get on top. I would agree immediately; I learned while at business school how important it is that both parties be able to see things from the other person's position.

I must admit that lying on those sopping rags was not the most comfortable of positions, but it was more than a fair trade-off for experiencing Liana's additional skills and seeing the ecstasy she could achieve from above. She'd mount me gently, then start pumping, sort of navigating our course around the floor. The best part of this arrangement was being able to look at her gorgeous tits as they dangled in my face. Okay, I'm probably biased, but they were absolutely beautiful with their warm, light brown tone highlighted by the thick, almost purplish nipples.

From below, I could reach up and take her breasts into my wet, sudsy palms, massaging them gently as she pumped her groin energetically on my cock. I'd start at the bottom, just stroking them with a pair of knuckles from both hands, then spread to full palms, taking the breasts first from the sides, then working my way to the top, then back down again.

Then I'd press my thumbs against her stiffened nipples, twirling them about while the rest of my fingers stroked the top half of her breasts. While this was going on, Liana would go crazy, pumping wildly and bringing herself to one, two and who-can-count-any-more orgasms. Her long, almost weeping squeal of rapture was the most fantastic thing I'd ever heard, and I'd often just grab her ass and join her in the rapture, sweeping into screaming orgasms.

The only problem with her up above was that a few times, we'd get so caught up in the heat of passion that she'd lower her tits right to my face. Instinctively, I'd raise my head a bit and start sucking on those gorgeous melons—only to get a rich, soapy taste filling my mouth. I'd then start choking and spitting out what I'd just sucked in and we'd have to separate and take a little breather until I recovered.

After her first couple of visits, I started giving her little presents every time she came down to clean. At first, they were fairly simple—some new sexy underwear, a box of chocolates—just small tokens of my appreciation. Before long, they got more elaborate—jewellery, a nice bag, designer underwear (none of which looked like ice kachang). As my little presents became more and more generous, Liana grew even more zealous in her cleaning. Sometimes the two of us would do the floor two or three times at one go, making it immaculate. Then she'd jump up, say she was late, rush in and shower, pull her clothes back on, give me a hurried kiss goodbye and rush out.

And, God, was she sweet. Often, just as we'd finished, while I was still lying on top of her, she'd look up and ask, "Are you really happy here with me, Sir Jeffrey?" And I would say yes, really. And then she'd lay her head back into a pool of blue foam and say, "Me too. I am so really happy. Really."

Towards the end of those two fabulous months, I made a major decision. I decided that I was going to make this thing permanent. I wanted to go up to Liana's employers and ask if we could make some deal whereby I could purchase her employment contract off them. I wanted her to be my maid full-time. Did not want to share her with anyone, not even some doddering old lady. But I didn't move immediately on this urge. I wanted to give it some time, maybe two weeks, mull it over, make sure I was making the right decision. That was my mistake, one of the biggest of my life. Before that two weeks was out, so was Liana—out of Singapore.

She didn't come as scheduled one day, and I was puzzled, well, a bit pissed-off actually. I tried without success to get in touch with her over the next few days and when I couldn't, I grew quite concerned. I tracked down some of her maid friends around the Chateau and asked if she was sick or something. No, they told me; she'd been sent back to Indonesia by her employers. Ma'am had apparently found some expensive items stashed in her room: earrings, bracelets, necklaces. The bitch accused Liana of having stolen them from somewhere. Liana insisted that they weren't stolen, they were presents. "Presents? From who?" asked Ma'am. Liana said they were from her boyfriend and admitted she had a boyfriend she snuck off and saw sometimes.

"Did she, uhh, ever say who this boyfriend was?" I asked. Her friends shrugged. Some guy from the construction site down the hill, they guessed, a Thai or a Bangladeshi. That's what she told her employers anyway. Of course, this merely confirmed for the couple that Liana was lying, that she had obviously stolen those articles; no foreign construction worker could ever in his wildest dreams have afforded such presents.

The friends went on to tell me that before they repatriated Liana, the couple had confiscated all of her fancy presents. They told the poor girl that since she wouldn't tell them the truth of where they came from, they were going to donate the gifts to some suitable charity. (Probably the dour bitch's Office Show-off Charity, I muttered to myself.)

One of the friends had managed to go to the airport with Liana when she was flown back. The poor thing had cried the whole time while waiting to board, according to this friend. She also kept insisting, over and over again, that she really had this boyfriend, really: a real, true boyfriend, kind and generous, cute even, the kind she had always dreamed about meeting. And then she did, and he had become her *real* boyfriend.

At this, I could only nod and choke out a few words. "Yeah, I believe her. I think she definitely had a real boyfriend. A girl as pretty and sweet as that, she could have had anyone she wanted. Really." I then thanked them for their help, said I had some things I had to attend to urgently, turned and rushed off. When I got back inside my apartment, I slammed my fist against the wall. And there was something harsh and stinging in my eyes for awhile.

Needless to say, my kitchen floor has never been so clean again. And I have never once since then known such pure, uncluttered happiness. Really.

Dancer From The Dance

Felix Cheong

The autumn gets to you on a Brisbane night like this. You walk and it trails. You sit and it sinks. You laugh and it breathes. Your warmth is its life.

Turning up your collar, you pace the sidewalk down Adelaide Street, rounding the corner at Queen Street Mall. Steps you have known like the back of your mind. A map rendered even in dreams.

She'll be there tonight, at Showgirls. Joanna's her name. A stripper with such abandon as only youth knows. The way she twists herself on the floor, flinging off clothes like cocoons. All of twenty, and everything a leap into the light. Oh, the madness of a human spectacle.

You must have seen her naked body many times, stomping to a rhythm you take home hours afterwards. You remember her smoothness and flaws as clearly as day, as if they were your own.

You must have touched her many times, those fifty-dollar lap dances that admit you into her crevices and clefts for a quarter of an hour. How your fingers search and relent, her breasts taut and warm, her hair long and blonde, a linger of lilac, the rose tattoo at rest on her shoulder blade, the reach of arms you have felt for needle marks.

Sometimes, she lets your hands pass between her thighs, as a bridge to the small of her back. But you are not turned on.

For this is not as real as it gets. You have to imagine yourself onto the set of *Exotica,* that Atom Egoyan film about strippers you love and must have restaged, shot by shot, in the cinema of your mind. This is not about stripping as sex but metaphor. This is about the lack when nothing else is left.

You have assumed the rank of Joanna's regular, a habit prompting her at nine o'clock each night. The other girls no longer treat you as bait. Palming a kiss as you descend into the swirl and sway of the club, she leads you to your favourite table.

You hold a man in the mirror for a spell but he turns away. His contempt is yours.

You like to think you're immune to the stuff, oh yeah.
But it's closer to the truth to say you can't get enough.
You know you're gonna have to face it, you're addicted
*   to love.*

On stage, Jessica is into the third song of her act, down to her white G-string, legs astride the pole, all platinum and tits. She tosses a wink which you accept. A dryness settles, but it's not something a gin and tonic can't help you forget.

"Have you been up there yet?"

"Yes. I'm always the first. You should know that."

The strangeness of familiarity, how you keep following the same conversation and don't recognise its footfalls. The muttering retreats.

Sometimes, you and Joanna wander among things that matter—pasts, cuts, hearts. The mornings before the clock winds down, before secrets become whispers. Most times, you wring the most out of things that don't—routes and routines that make and take up half of living.

"You want a lap dance tonight?"

"Hmm ... let me sip on it. Give me two good reasons."

"Well, there're no good reasons."

Trust her to tell it like it is. Her voice dips like a drowning in and out of the music—it must be early '90s House—but that's really all you need, or want. Her presence as a type, an image, a foil to what has been generating and gathering inside your mind for some time now.

That you are somehow the testing ground, a battlefield between morality and writing. That when one is not tested, the other must be trite. No wisdom without dirt.

You have shown her your clutch of poems that light no candle as you watch her read about yourself. A smile is as much a comment. And you wonder, when your language has finally been used and flung, worn out and hung, like a rag, a bone—what remains?

"What are you thinking about? You're quiet tonight."

And here she is, your experience, your muse, a vivacious young woman daring you. But your eyes say little next to hers.

"Oh, nothing. Well, things. Just thinking about things."

You leave it to the beat to absorb the silence. On stage, another stripper is strutting her stuff, her guts—Heidi, not an hour past eighteen, straining her eyes some distance into the dark. Ten weeks into the job and she's already cool to the catcalls and clawing eyes.

Joanna flits to another table, another customer dressed like you, picking up the scent of money, a half-finished conversation that might make her night worth the while.

Your eyes tailgate them to a corner, she leading him by the hand. The music whips into another frenzy, cascading upon loss and your words, like her clothes, plugging holes on the downbeat.

Night At
Passion Touch

Hari Kumar

I open the door of my flat and step into my living room. It suddenly looks small and depressing. And lifeless. In this little slot in the sky, I am nothing more than a claustrophobic pigeon. Depression rules me within these four walls, which seem to be inching closer day by day like a sinister army, a tightening noose. My tiny apartment is known by the number 15–75, which fills me with a deep longing for homes that had names, religions, moods, ghosts, personalities, attitude … Here the walls creep in, the furniture grows, the air rots and silence splits my head slooowly. My block is a giant filing cabinet. Of people filed away to be forgotten.

In the last few months after my estranged wife Nisha had got this job she would be travelling often, leaving me within these carnivorous walls to get hypnotised by the TV. Not that Nisha was great company; our home had become an art-house movie in the recent months, with monosyllables hanging in the air like the Sumatran haze. But she was a presence nevertheless. She was a scent, a grunt, a flash of colour, a shuffle of feet, a word, an incomplete line ... We spoke through Post-it Notes on the fridge.

When the TV became unbearable I got drawn into the Internet. Like God, I had 108 names in the many chat rooms I stalked. Like God, I could become male, female, genderless. Like God, I felt powerful, omnipotent. But the topic was always the same. The people were always sick. And the world was such a fake. I soon got sick of it and wondered how anyone could be addicted to this cyber-madness.

Of course, there were the plus points of the Internet, like email and free pornography. But then again, my email account started receiving more and more spam than regular mails. Daily emails promised me fourteen inches of masculinity; all-I-can-eat Viagra; a thousand "sure-fire" ways to make money, lose weight, grow younger, get out of debt, etc. Even the pornography became boring. There are only so many ways the human anatomy can be arranged and juxtaposed. To me, the Internet was just a shooting star.

So when the television and the Internet died their deaths in me, I started wandering after work, in order to avoid the frozen shadows of home as much as possible. I drove past the seedy underbelly of Singapore: places like Geylang, Desker, or Changi Village where the transsexuals were prettier and curvier than the female prostitutes. But that was as far as I could go with those night creatures.

But the massage parlours, "health centres" as they were euphemistically called, were a different thing altogether. Since most of them were located in shopping malls, they bore a façade of respectability. My first such "healthy" experience was in a massage centre in the fourth floor of a shopping mall off Orchard Road. For almost a week, I had been loitering around the mall mustering up the courage to open that door of Passion Touch Health Centre. On that night I had downed two pegs of whiskey at a nearby pub, so I had some courage flowing fast through my veins.

After spending twenty long minutes gazing at the lingerie on a mannequin in a boutique next to the health centre and getting some dirty looks from the boutique's salesgirl in the process, I held my breath and turned the door knob of Passion Touch. The opening of the door immediately set off some kind of chime that startled me for a moment and made me want to run away. The brightly lit lobby, though small, was, to my surprise, quite plush and even pleasant. I had expected a dark and dingy place with women hanging in the shadows, smouldering cigarettes between their lips.

The cheerful old lady behind the reception desk was watching a Channel 8 Chinese drama from a small wall-mounted TV beside the door. She looked at me and gave me a very bright, "Hallowelcome." She opened a register and asked me to write my name and identity card number. I hesitated for a moment, feeling suspicious as to whether this was some kind of a blackmail racket. "No worry, lah," the lady said, slapping my arm. "You so malu, hor. Everyone write, see. You go any health centre, also write." She flipped the pages to show me lines and lines of scribbles, most of them unintelligible. I scribbled "D. Nair," and for my IC number, I jumbled up three digits. Thankfully, she didn't bother to ask for my identity card.

"You first time, haah?" She gave me a motherly smile.

"First time in Singapore," I said proudly, pushing out my chest and placing my arms on my hips. "I go London, Paris, New York, Bangkok. Everywhere I go massage," I said, looking at her over the tip of my nose.

"You tourist, haah?"

I nodded impatiently.

"So how come you have IC number?" she asked, narrowing her eyes.

"Um ... I ... I ... That's my passport number," I blurted out finally.

She nodded understandingly, then added, "For tourists, thirty dollars extra, hor. So, seventy dollars."

I cursed myself under my breath and placed a fifty and two tens on the desk.

"Wait, hor. I call masseuse," she said, putting on a toothy smile. As I waited, I took a good look at the lobby. In a niche in the wall were three large porcelain statues of Fu, Lu and Shou, the Taoist gods for happiness, wealth and longevity. They seemed to be looking at me with a what-a-stupid-boy-you-are expression. I ignored them and shifted my gaze to the high Chinese altar made of blood-red rosewood on which stood a few burning joss sticks emitting a thick scent and lazy fumes that rose up to the ceiling. Behind those joss sticks was a large statue, also porcelain, of Qwan Yin, the goddess of mercy, sitting on a giant lotus and holding a small vase on her lap. On her face was an expression of such equanimity that it disturbed me and prompted me to look away.

Within minutes, another woman who looked like the old hag's elder sister appeared. The woman was fat, ugly as well.

"She, Jane, your masseuse," the reception hag told me brightly, pointing to the fat woman.

I looked at her, wide-eyed, from top to bottom. "I ... ermm ... I ... um ... Can you get me someone younger? If you please?" I asked politely, while—in my mind—I said, "She Jane or maybe Jane's elephant, but I no Tarzan, lor. Gimme someone young and soft for my young and soft muscles, alamak!"

"She vely good! Vely vely experience," the receptionist said.

"I can see she is 'vely experienced.' But please ... No offence ... but, I want someone younger," I said firmly.

The two exchanged something fast in Hokkien. Jane looked at me blankly and disappeared inside. "Hokay," the receptionist said finally, "I give you vely chio ger. Vely young. But cost thirty dollar extra, hokay?"

For a moment, I was shocked and didn't know what to say. But having come this far, I was not going back without the "passion touch" of young, girlie hands. I nodded, halfheartedly, and placed three crisp ten-dollar notes on the desk. She pocketed them and said, "Good. You wait for thirty minutes, hor. She no here. I telephone," she picked up the phone.

"You go in. Make comfortable. Sauna, TV all inside. Jane show you. Jane make Chinese tea for you," she said, covering the mouthpiece.

Jane appeared again and led me through a narrow corridor,

which had numbered doors on either side. She opened door Number 8 for me and handed me a large, freshly laundered white towel. "You take shower, change towel and wait. You want moe towel, inside cubberd. I bling Chinese tea. You want sauna, TV, you go end colido, turn light," she said, motioning with her right hand.

The room was small and dimly lit with a clean single bed in the middle. There was a cupboard placed against one of the walls and another door, which I guessed led to the attached bathroom. Although the air was stale and reeked of dampness, the room was clean. I closed the door, undressed and, after wrapping the towel around me, stepped into the bathroom. I was initially a bit reluctant in touching the towel—you never know what things it may have been used to wipe off. But then, it appeared clean and crisp and felt nice in my hands. Luckily, there was a fresh bar of soap in the bathroom; the tiny type you find in hotels.

I had a leisurely bath; the water was hot and refreshing. By the time I stepped out of the bathroom, there was a cup of hot Chinese tea waiting for me. I hung the wet towel in the bathroom towel rack, took a dry one from the cupboard, and wrapped it around my midriff. The hot tea helped in warming me up since I was finding the air conditioning inside the room too chilly for my skin.

By the time I finished my tea, there was a knock on the door, and before I could say "Come in!", the door swung open and in came one of the prettiest Chinese things I have seen in Singapore. At that moment, all my feelings of having been fleeced out of my hard-earned money vanished in a trice. She could have been mistaken for a Shenton Way babe except for her skirt, which showed too much thigh for a bank teller.

She crushed her cigarette butt in the ashtray and gave me a sweet, "Hello-how-are-you-I-am-Linda-oil-or-powder?"

"What?" I gaped at her.

"Oil or powder. For massage, you want oil or powder?" she replied with amused eyes.

"Oil," I said.

From the cupboard, she took out a bottle of baby oil and gestured for me to lie on the bed. I lay on my stomach and became like a lump of chapathi dough in her hands. She started kneading me, and I started needing her. Ooh so badly! I moaned like I had never moaned before. "Aaaahhh ... that's it ... yesssss ... ooohh ... a little to the left ... that's the point ... hmmm ..."

And she was going like, "Good muscles ... not too much ... not too little ..."

"What's your name?" she asked casually.

"James Bond," I replied. She giggled.

She removed my towel with an expert flick and started on my buttocks and thighs.

"You married?"

"James Bond's not married," I replied.

She pinched my butt.

"Ow! Hope I don't have to pay extra for that."

She giggled again. "You're a joker ... You're also a liar."

"And you speak good English for a Passion Touch girl."

"Was a remisier once upon a time ... with the Midas touch ... earning big bucks ..." She applied light karate chops on my thighs with both her hands.

"Aaah … that feels good …" I said, letting off a sigh of pleasure.

"Now a masseur … with Passion Touch … earning big fucks," she said with a chuckle and quickly added, "Have no regrets anyway. Now turn over."

I turned over and lay on my back. She deftly laid the towel over my middle. I looked at her straight. The dim ceiling light was behind her head and I couldn't make out the look on her face. She leaned closely to massage my chest after sprinkling oil on it. Her hair fell on my face. I could smell her shampoo mingled with a faint scent of sweat. Garlic sweat.

"So what'll it be? Hand job, blow, sandwich or the full course?" she asked; her tone was very professional.

"Sandwich," I said confidently, although I wasn't quite sure what she meant. I felt like a snack anyway.

"That'll be forty dollars extra, okay," she said softly.

"That's one expensive sandwich!" I thought, and swallowed spit. But I didn't want to give her the impression I was a cheapskate. So I nodded my head impatiently and asked her to get on with it.

She lifted my towel like a magician lifts the cloth over the caged bird. She took one look at my manhood and said, "Now I know why you called yourself James Bond: that's a nought-nought-seven-inch — nought-nought much!" she giggled.

"Nought-nought little either," I said crossly.

"Just kidding. Don't worry, you're average," she said, taking off her clothes. In no time, she was stark naked. She wore absolutely nothing under her natty outfit. She had a slim body with perky tits—very playful, like twin puppies, jiggling at the slightest movement, topped by tiny cherry nipples. Her skin was like milk.

She unscrewed the spout on the bottle of oil, poured a generous amount on my chest and applied it thickly all over. Then she handed me the bottle and said, "Now it's your turn."

I raised myself to a sitting position and poured a handful of oil into my cupped hand. I then applied the oil on her chest and stomach. She gently pushed me back onto the bed, whispering, "Lie, you liar."

She then lay on me, skin on oily skin, like two slithering snakes. "No sex, okay. Only touch touch. For sex, my rate is a hundred."

Hundred bucks for a blasted fuck! I knew my wallet had only a fifty-dollar note. Not this time anyway, I thought. "Not that I don't have the money, but I think I will pass this time," I said.

She looked at me but said nothing. She hugged me tight and continued rubbing her body on mine. Her breath came hot on my lips. I could catch the whiff of Fisherman's Friend mints, apple and cinnamon, I guess. Her hair fell around my face like a black curtain. My whole body tingled with sensations never felt before. Primal moans rose in my throat. Down below, I was hard as rock. Feeling my hardness, she asked breathlessly, "Do you want sex?"

"Do you ... take Visa?" I asked between gasps.

"Cash ... only cash,"

"But …"

"Yeah … many others do, but we don't … Never mind," she said, getting up, "There's always a next time."

"But where's my sandwich?" I asked innocently as she was putting her clothes back on.

She looked at me blankly before saying, "Oh! I forgot to tell you—usually a sandwich massage is an oily guy between two girls. But I didn't think you wanted to lie on top of Jane. After all, you're only James Bond, not Tarzan," she chuckled.

"Oh yes—the *sandwich* massage!" I exclaimed. Suddenly things were a lot clearer.

She gave me another blank look and said, "My time is up. Forty dollars please." A month later, I rang up Passion Touch and asked for Linda.

"She go Austalia. Myglate myglate. With *ang moh* boyflend," the reception hag said.

On The Sofa

Kirpal Singh

The sofa is always very good, you said
Firm and soft at the same time
And, don't forget, flexible—
Allows men of your age to manoeuvre

Men of my age? How many had you had?
The mind refuses to entertain truths
Linked to hot afternoons on sofas

Don't worry, dear, you added,
Smoothly caressing the growing finale
It's not the number but the memory
And I don't remember most …

Of course you meant that as a compliment
And lying beneath your writhing assured
Even as we rocked the floorboards
In the end only memories are left.

Two Men
And A Plan

O Thiam Chin

"We are not the products of our circumstances, but we are surely the sum of all the stupid choices that our parents have inflicted on us." Shun told me this when he took me to my first client.

"And there is nothing we can do to undo this damage—not you, not me," he added emphatically.

Shun liked to spout pop-psychology babble like this, off the top of his head, given any opportunity. He spoke freely, without any fear of consequences, and he was not afraid of offending anyone. Least of all me.

How he derived all these sage-sounding maxims that he liked to toss around so much was well beyond me. But he did tell me once that he enjoyed reading the works of writers like Douglas Coupland and Chuck Palahniuk because, according to him, they tell truths—"dark sickening truths of our depraved times"—that other writers are incapable or unwilling to write about. How true that was, I did not know. I hated to read. Beyond the textbooks and all the assigned reading materials given out by my lecturers and tutors each week, I barely had time for other forms of reading, nor did I read for leisure. I considered it a waste of time. I had better things to do.

"And treat this client well, you hear? Big fish like him are hard to find, especially since he's paying top dollar for a virgin like you," Shun said in jest, throwing a snickering look in my direction.

"Fuck you," I replied caustically.

"I don't think so tonight, my dear. He—" Shun emphasised the word, while pointing to the hotel door in front of us, "will be fucking you tonight. And do everything he says. He says fuck, you fuck. He says suck, you suck. He wants to rim you, by all means, spread your legs wider and let him rim. Don't say no, don't ever, or we'll lose him. Remember, it's easier to retain an existing client than scout for ten new ones." Shun grinned at me and gestured for me to knock on the door.

I hated him when he spun out this kind of tough talk, like I was the novice and he was the professional. As if this was my first time fucking or sucking or rimming. Fucker. But on a deeper level, I knew that I did not want to disappoint him nor be angry with him for long. I hated this mixed feeling, this anger combined with an eagerness to please him and do what he said. I hated to admit it because I knew exactly why I reacted in this way. Because I knew that I had grown to like Shun a lot. Damn it, damn me.

"I'll pick you up when you're done, or when he's done with you. Give me a call later," Shun said, flashing me his killer smile and nudging me again to knock on the door.

Before I could say anything more to him, he had turned and begun to walk away, down the quiet corridor towards the lift. I stood and watched him saunter away from me. He turned the corner and disappeared from my sight.

I stared at the room door—235—and gathered my random thoughts. This was not my first time fucking another guy, so why was I feeling this way? This dreaded sense of inevitability? Had I made a wrong choice here? And if so, why did I agree to Shun's idea in the first place?

I took in a breath, and felt the sharp intake of air lifting away some of my anxieties. I knocked on the door. It opened almost immediately and I entered the hotel room.

I was cruising in one of the toilets in the university hostel where I was staying when Shun first saw me. Right away, my sight was on him, this handsome and darkly tanned man, muscular in an athletic way. My lust went into high alert instantly, mounting all my senses into full force. Of course, I had seen him around on campus; it was hard not to notice him, with his clean-cut good looks, which no doubt attracted attention from women and men alike. Well, gay men, in any case.

Being in such close proximity with him, in the toilet, I grabbed my chance. I tried to arouse his attention with an obvious look of lust and longing. He was washing his hands, but I could tell he was aware that I was looking hard at him, getting his attention. He glanced in my direction and caught my lingering stare, my intentional body signals. He did not look surprised or puzzled by my actions, nor did he walk away with an unhidden disgust, as some would when faced with people like me in the public toilets or changing rooms. Instead, he walked over to me in a fume.

"What are you looking at?" he asked angrily. He stood inches away from my heated face, his words coming at me with unbridled force. I looked away guiltily, cursing inwardly for trying to hook the wrong guy. But Shun pressed on, his angry words building up to a crescendo.

"You make me sick! All day long, hanging around in public toilets, in school, at the pools, anywhere, waiting with that cock-hungry look, eager to suck on any cock that comes along the way. You pathetic fuckers—get a life!"

His words came out in a torrent while his intense gaze continued to remain on me. My body began to tremble visibly, as my own words choked in my throat. I wanted to say something, anything, in return, but I did not. I was scared somehow. I did not want to be caught like this and the shame of being trapped in this awkward situation only ate at me relentlessly, building up to an unbearable degree.

I quickly gathered up the courage to walk briskly away and head for the exit. But Shun stopped me abruptly on my way out and demanded to have my details. "Give me your hostel room number; if not, I'll report you to the dean," he threatened. In the heat of being caught, exposed and threatened, I did as he told me. I gave him my hostel room number without a second thought and left the toilet hurriedly.

That night, Shun knocked on door and I let him in. He fucked me without saying a word and I became his secret friend.

Naturally, I wanted to ask him about his outburst during our first meeting in the toilet. But I kept quiet as I was afraid of upsetting him and did not want to appear too forward, lest he drop me after a few fucks. Basically, I had to acknowledge he was a great fuck and there were not many like him around, at least not in the university. The weekend sex in town always seemed so far away, especially with my schoolwork and projects with looming deadlines; to have Shun nearby for a quick fuck was more than I could ask for.

So after that first night he fucked me, and the night that followed, I let him have his way with me, whichever way he wanted me. And he came every night for the whole week, always around eight, when my roommate was in the library poring through his school texts or assignments till late at night. Shun kept absolutely quiet throughout the fucking. And I followed his lead and kept quiet. I did not want to spoil anything between us at this stage.

"Sometimes you really make me sick. Always hanging around some pathetic toilet, waiting for some cock to appear."

We had agreed to meet for lunch at the canteen after our lectures. Shun majored in Mechanical Engineering in National Technological University, where he was in his final year, while I was in my second year in the same engineering faculty, taking Computer Sciences.

Shun was in a good mood that day, going through his litany of complaints about me. This was four months after we first met in my hostel toilet.

"You can never stop, can you?" Shun asked in a tone that preempted any reply from me. Not that I had anything to say in return. All that he had said was true, in some sense. I cruised for sex and I sucked cocks. It was simple as that, and Shun knew and was able to exploit it. It was hard to change one's nature, and Shun knew this well.

And he knew where he stood in the gay food chain and wanted to remain there, among those in the upper echelon, feasting and preying on those below him. A vicious cycle of man-eating-man within the gay world. And he knew how to make the most of his looks to give him what he wanted, in any circumstance. He refused to be the product of his circumstances, a fate and state that he abhorred, because, to him, "… it rules out the possibility—or certainty—of free will and the stupid choices that made us who we are." And so he stuck to his self–made logic and beliefs.

"Since you are always so cock-hungry, then learn to make use of this desire for your own advantage, to gain something for yourself, not just swallow what comes along the way."

I gave him a blank look and a disgusted cluck of the tongue. Shun saw my look of contempt but ignored it completely and continued, "What I'm saying is this: since you are still young, only twenty-three and not bad-looking, you can use these god-given attributes and your superb cock-sucking skill for some gains, to reap the benefits of your youth, so to speak. To keep it simple: Let sex and money go hand in hand, that's what I'm saying."

I was not surprised by his suggestion since I had known for

some time that Shun had been a rent boy for a while—since his junior college days, in fact. While Shun did not spell out exactly what he was doing, he had dropped strong hints about this "freelance job" he had which allowed him to pay for his school fees and some "small luxuries." From what I could gather from our conversations and see with my own eyes, he was being way too humble about how lucrative this job could be. He was earning tons from his so-called freelance work, as far as I could tell. Shun did not hesitate to pay for the meals we had, the movies, the clothes and bags that I wanted, my school fees, my allowance. He relished being "the provider," he told me once after we had sex, "unlike my father, who ran away with his mistress, leaving nothing for me and my mother." When I tried to inquire more about his family background, he grew very still and quiet, lying like a stranger beside me in the dark. And that was when I knew never to ask him again about his family. I would let him tell me what he wanted to reveal, if he chose to, but I could never ask him for details or any questions of that sort.

"So you want me to be like you?" I said mockingly, enunciating each word slowly.

"Yes, and I'll be your mentor or something. Your daddy pimp, so to speak."

"You? So what's in it for you? What will you gain?"

"Fifty-fifty for the first few times. After that, seventy-thirty, you seventy, me thirty. How's that?"

"Sounds fair. But how are you going to find the clients?"

"That's for me to worry about." Shun smiled at me

disarmingly, as if hoarding a common secret of which I had no knowledge, and I was briefly agitated by his cocksure attitude.

"In case you are so blind and haven't noticed, living in that little world of yours," he pointed to my head with wry off-handedness, "there are plenty of rich old faggots around who're dying for some companionship and a quick fuck now and then. And we'll give them just that, a good fuck. Their money for the sex we give. A fair transaction."

While I disagreed with Shun on many occasions, what he had just said made plenty of good sense. In a way, he dared to put into words what went on in his head and was able to justify his actions with his own concocted motives and convictions. I would have failed to see—or maybe refused to acknowledge—these basic human needs of love and sex. Clear knowledge was not something I wanted to hold onto, I found it too cumbersome, a burden. But the fact that we are all lonely and always craving for some form of companionship, to the extent of being willing to pay anything for someone to love, to hold even for a short while, all these rang true to me.

I did not answer him; what could I say to what he had just told me? How much of it was true, how much of it was fabricated by him? I did not know. I had never paid for sex nor had I been paid for sex. Most of the sex I ever had up to then had been the anonymous, cruising-in-the-toilet kind. Of course, I was vaguely aware that there was a dark, seedy side to the sex trade, but I was never that curious to find out more. But Shun knew that world well and was willing to share his knowledge with me. He wanted to be my friend and pimp. So I listened to him like a young protégé learning the ways of the world.

Shun kept his word and let me keep the money I earned, after the fifth time he introduced me to a new client. Though at that point, I was not hard up for money, as I had developed a steady flow of regular clients that patronised me. After the initial meeting, they would come back to me for more and I would always agree to every request. Why say no to good money? I reminded myself constantly, and slowly I was convinced of the validity of what I had said.

"Keep the rates fixed," Shun reminded me for the first few times. "And don't change them at all. It's in the best interest of both you and your clients."

Within a few months, I was already getting the hang of the trade, of what needed to be done or was expected from Shun and the clients that he introduced me to. Shun would scout out prospective clients: some were his old clients, some he found through his ingenious means of contact, which he kept hidden from me. Given the secrecy that governed this kind of sex, still banned in Singapore and subject to criminal prosecution, I was genuinely surprised and mildly curious how Shun managed to find these contacts.

He once told me, when we were having dinner in a shopping centre food court in Jurong after our economics classes, that guys would often approach him in gay clubs on the weekends and chat him up. Slowly they would express their interest in knowing him more, some blatant or bold enough might even suggest some action for later. Of course, Shun would assess each person according to his own criteria, which were quite simple actually: he must be rich; he must own at least a Lexus, Mercedes or Porsche; he must live by himself in some District 9 or 10 apartment; and he must hold a high senior-management position in some big-shot company. These criteria were non-negotiable, he said, otherwise one might compromise and lose out in the end. Shun reminded me countless times that I was in it for their money, not for some fucking relationship or friendship.

"They do not care about you—that is why they'd rather pay for sex than invest their time and effort in finding somebody to build a reasonable relationship with. These people do not have the time for such things and that is the reason why we exist. We provide them with the one-stop centre where they can purchase companionship, sex and cheap feelings for a premium price. It is a fair deal."

As he said these things, Shun's eyes would often glint with a self-satisfied concentration, as if he had set everything in place and nothing would go wrong. To him, our freelance work was based on a supply-and-demand fulfillment of human needs. The nature and practicality of what we were doing could be set down in simple workable rules and a positive mindset. The ABCs of the gay sex trade, so to speak.

Shun was amoral, and he lived by what he believed in. "Nothing is impossible if you put your mind to it," he would say, spouting a dead wise man's often-repeated, dead-of-meaning axiom. But he also had his own salubrious blend of half-fucked ideas and self-thought-out rules of gay life.

I told him once, "Maybe you should write a book, be the voice of our generation, start a new sexual revolution here in Singapore, break new fucking frontiers for us disenfranchised and delusional faggots. Perhaps people would take note of us. We would be the mainstream and they, these normal heterosexual fucks, would finally be sidelined and marginalised, a sideshow of freaks preserving their straight traditions and way of life." But Shun just shot me a what-the-hell-are-you-talking-about look, as if I was the biggest idiot in this world and my words were all one-cent coins—useless, worth nothing.

"And why the hell would I do this? To tell the big fucking world about what we are doing? The bloody reason why we are able to do well, to get the clients we are getting now, be paid obscenely for our sex, is because we—our deeds, are kept hidden, away from the public eye and this secrecy grants us greater value. Because we are scarce, 'at a premium,' we are always in demand."

"Don't think too much about what you're doing. And cut the Pretty Woman crap about not kissing on the lips, okay? It was embarrassing when I called Gabriel to check with him and he told me about this. When did you devise this romantic-crap stuff? Too much movies in your head."

Shun and I were heading for our morning lectures at the university and he was admonishing me on what I had done wrong during the latest weekend assignment. Walking up the stairs towards the lecture theatre at eight forty-five on a cloudy, lazy Monday after a tiring three-tryst weekend, I was far from being awake or alert. But I listened anyway, nodding my head to what Shun had to say, paying what little attention I could muster.

As I listened to him, I looked around at the other students walking alongside us, heading for their respective classes, carrying their haversacks and files of notes, looking fresh and bright eyed. Some were munching on their breakfasts of buttered toast or freshly cut-up fruit, fiddling with packets of coffee or iced Milo; others were talking animatedly on their mobiles, checking on after-class gatherings with their classmates, making lunch appointments with their friends. I wondered what kind of lives they had, what after-school activities they might pursue. Did they, too, have secret lives they kept from their close friends? Did they have sex three times last weekend and earn almost three thousand dollars from it? Would they share this secret with anyone, if they had the chance to do so? Would they be ashamed?

As I stole quick glances at their faces, I realised how far I was from their way of life, their seemingly normal lifestyle of blind dates, late-night movies, furtive kisses, crushes or cramming for tests. I would never be like them, and I was half relieved and half scared by this fact. Half relieved because I did not want to be hiding from what I was, from my sexuality and my needs. Half scared because I was heading nowhere and was fearful of being ostracised by my peers, my family and the whole damn society.

Like any pimp worth his salt, Shun wanted to make sure I got the machinations of this trade into my head, and so he kept drilling these words into me, until I could repeat them word for word. By then, I was already onto my eleventh rich client.

"Just be careful in what you do or what the client wants. Always wear a condom and insist on one if he wants to fuck. Be persistent and show that you are in control over this matter. And never give in to bareback sex. Trust me, you don't want to die from AIDS at your age. It won't be the best experience of your life."

I nodded like a puppet and agreed with what he said. "How long?" I had wanted to ask him several times before, but could not drum up any courage to do so. "Why did you go into this line? Was there no other way?" But I knew he would not entertain my questions.

His secret life as a rent boy was known only to me. "Why me?" I wanted to ask. Did his friends know anything about this life at all? Each time I saw him with his classmates or close friends, in the canteen or library or at the swimming pool, he would look away, ignoring me completely. He would feign that nothing was out of sorts and carry on the conversations with his friends, joking and laughing with them. And every time I would be hurt by his careless actions, no matter how hard I tried not to think about it.

But when he was with me, away from his friends, he displayed a completely different side of himself: a serious no-nonsense Shun, in control of himself and me as well. How could I ever confront him with this disparity? His eccentric behaviour? He had every reason to back away from me, to head back to his normal life, to have anything and everything he wanted— great looks, peer admiration, good grades, and an attractive personality. What did I have that I could give him? My mouth and my ass? He could have that from anyone, anytime, so why me?

Slowly, Shun began to share other aspects of his secret life with me. About the middle-aged banker who wanted to keep him as a toy-boy and almost bought him a condominium and a car. But Shun turned him down flatly "because he has a wife and two kids, and there are too many fucking complications."

And about the creative director of a US-based international advertising agency, who wanted more than just normal sex: "He's such a pervert and jerk, always asking me to do this and that to him, pull off the S&M acts on him. But it's hilarious, some of the things he's asked me to do." Or about a rich Indonesian-Chinese guy, who claimed to love him and wanted Shun to be his boyfriend: "You should be there, to hear him say the things he says. Taken straight from some trashy magazines or C-grade romance novels. Lovable, but too clingy."

Where Shun got some of this clientele, I did not know and really did not care to know. But it bothered me to no end, to know that he was with these strange men, let alone having sex with them. And so I didn't ask him anything about them.

I should have seen it coming sooner or later. Shun was planning to leave me on my own. We had been good friends, but our friendship was not something that could be carried along in our own separate lives. It would be incongruous, even absurd. Of course, by then, I already had a small but growing pool of clients generating a steady flow of comfortable income.

"Do you know what I've been doing? Teaching you everything that I have learnt through my mistakes, bad experiences and weird encounters? It's not about the money. It's about strengthening your guts and mind." Shun looked straight into my face, saying these words with a controlled demeanour, his eyes intensely lucid. "When I first saw you in the toilet, all I saw was a pitiable creature, crawling around on his fours, looking so helpless and lost, and I was so angry. 'Why are you doing this to yourself?' I wanted to ask, 'Being at the mercy of the next person who comes into the toilet and gives you a sympathetic fuck.' And I wanted so much to grab you there and then and give you a sound beating."

I bit my lower lip so hard, it began to bleed slightly. Was this true? Was I so helpless? But I did not want his sympathy, and I hated his pity.

"But why me? I'm sure you can take your pity to someone else. Why me then? Am I your personal charity case?" I shot out vehemently, tripping over my own words, and as I heard them coming out of my mouth, I could feel the helplessness of it. I stared at him as coldly as I could, in silent defiance.

"I don't know why. I don't know why I've chosen you. I just did," Shun replied, as he stirred his cup of mocha latte continuously, absent-mindedly, as if to blend his words into the murky mix. And he remained silent, his thoughts far away from mine, a world apart though we were sitting face to face in the Starbucks outlet in the university. The white noise of chatter and laughter from nearby tables drifted over in wisps. A young female student laughed heartily at the next table. A fly landed on

Shun's hand and he waved it away.

"I have an important client tonight who is organising a small orgy and wants the company of young men like us." Shun looked into my face for any changes, and seeing no expression, continued with his proposal.

"He's paying four thousand dollars for just one night. I want you to come along with me, we can split the money equally. Anyway, it's good money."

He stirred up the dregs of his drink with his straw, took a sip and pushed the cup away rudely, as if it was an abhorrent object he'd just discovered. I'd already taken part in several orgies by this time, so I was not squeamish about his request. But I wanted to refuse him, for the very sake of saying no to him, to deny him my dumb submission for once. But something in me, a pure rush of impulses, wanted to give in without hesitation. There was no reason to refuse him but there was no reason to acquiesce either.

"Come on, tell me, are you interested or not? If not, forget about it. Forget what I just said." With that, he pulled back his seat and stood up. My heart leapt to follow him.

"Okay, okay, I'm in. Just tell me where and when. I will be there," I said.

"I will call you later," Shun replied casually, before grabbing his bag hanging from the seat, smiled at me and left the table. A heavy feeling overcame me and, like a ship's anchor dropped into the depths, I was submerged and sunken.

The man answered the door almost immediately, as if he had

been standing behind it, waiting anxiously for our arrival. He extended his hand solicitously and welcomed us.

"Hi, you're finally here! We've been waiting! My name is Ben." With that, he gestured us into the spacious living room of his bungalow. "For a while, we thought you guys were lost," Ben said as he led us into the room. Which was almost impossible, I mused inwardly, since the bungalow stood apart from the rest of the houses along this stretch of road in the obsequiousness of its lavish façade. No one with eyes could miss it. In any case, Shun and I took a taxi from our hostel. Along the journey, we hardly talked to each other, except to ask the perfunctory questions. Shun looked out his window at passing streetlights, at people waiting at bus stops, at the traffic, hardly acknowledging my presence, while I stole long glances at him from time to time.

But upon entering the house, Shun quickly reverted to his amiable, almost businesslike self, a stark contrast to his other self, five minutes ago. He took the initiative to answer all the questions posed by Ben with an old-school-friend candour.

The house was sparsely decorated and furnished, with Postmodern paintings hanging on several walls and a large faux-fur carpet covering the living room floor. A few men sitting on the couch looked up as we approached. There were three of them, smartly dressed in polo shirts and pants, drinking red wine, their faces slightly flushed. Like Ben, they were in their late thirties, professional looking, cultured and very loaded. The last bit of information was supplied by Shun when he called me that afternoon to inform me of the details of this orgy. All of them stood and began to introduce themselves. After which, one of the men, Chris, offered Shun and me each a glass of Pinot Noir.

We sat and began to chat. Shun turned to talk to the guy closest to him, a music company vice president named Tim, while I made chit-chat with Chris, an art gallery owner. While we talked, Ben and his live-in boyfriend Stan pulled away from us and began to whisper to one another animatedly, after which Ben turned to address the rest of the group.

"Guys, since we are all here, I don't think we should waste any more time," Ben remarked with a wink before adding, "Let's go up to the room, shall we?"

With that, he grabbed hold of Stan's hand and began to lead the way. Chris, Tim and Shun stood up promptly and followed the two men. I held back momentarily, as the effects of the wine hit me. Shun looked back at me cursorily with a baleful frown. I got to my feet unsteadily and joined the group, my head pounding with spikes of brightness.

The bedroom was on the second floor of the house, at the further end. It was dimly lit with the warm orangish hues given off by two aluminum-cast table lamps. Stepping into the tepid room, I felt a rush of claustrophobia, as if the space had suddenly shrunk and was pressing in on all sides, pushing all of us together into this confining place. I drew in several inaudible breaths and oriented myself, trying to get a stable bearing. Ben and Stan had already stripped off their tops and were sandwiching Shun in their embrace, nudging him to take off his T-shirt, assisting him gently. Shun allowed them to strip him without any resistance. Meanwhile, Tim and Chris had surrounded me and were doing likewise, tugging at my shirt, undressing me as they moved their hungry hands over my body, as if appraising something they had just bought.

While they were undressing me, I looked over at the *ménage à trois* of Shun, Ben and Stan. By now, all of them were naked. With Shun between them, Ben and Stan were pressing their erections against his slender, muscular body, as they kissed his face and shoulders voraciously, like hunters savouring their prey. Shun seemed to luxuriate in their passion, perhaps even enjoying himself; I couldn't tell. As Shun kissed Ben full on his lips, he looked over at me piercingly. And with that look, I knew instinctively what he had been trying to convey for so long. He belonged to no one, not even me with my attraction and attachment. He refused to be claimed by anyone; no one should own him in any way. He chose to be free and his freedom created a wide chasm, uncrossable and unbridgeable.

A new wave of pain inundated me, numbing all my faculties and rendering them temporarily inoperative. I was devastated and dazed. But I had no time to think right then, with the hands of Chris and Tim all over me, caressing eagerly. I shut down my mind and gave myself over to them. I sought out Chris's mouth from the tangle of our bodies and kissed him hungrily. I did not hold back this time.

And Then She Came

Jonathan Lim

And then she came.

Across the wet grass between the dormitory blocks, heralding herself with a strident, indrawn wail like the sound of darkness laughing.

If any of the wakeful inmates heard her, they did not look up. If they had seen, they would not have dared to believe. Only he knew.

For she was coming to him.

The tree outside his dorm window shuddered, shaking off a night fragrance that was not its own—a scent pungent to the point of rot.

The boy lay naked on his bed, knowing there was no point in being anywhere else. She would have him there and had been violent getting him there on previous nights; he did not wish to extend the struggle or invite her wrath. Her affection was terrible enough.

One night, months ago, returning late from a party where he had drunk *almost* too much, he'd glimpsed her—a pale stranger, standing on the edge of a dark field. Not sober enough to be superstitious, he had lingered and looked. As he ogled, overstepping curiosity and forgetting caution, his as-yet-untried manhood swelled with lecherous urges. Then he had stumbled on his way.

But she had sensed him. Had heard his unworded lust, felt his molesting thoughts as he passed into the night.

And she had responded.

Every night since.

Every single night since, he had refused all engagements, denied all company, in order to be in his room at this time, in his bed, waiting for her to come and claim him and take her pleasure.

He no longer even bothered to stay clothed. He knew how she wanted him and no longer had any desire to appear otherwise when she arrived. Her will was like white-hot iron—everything melted and cleaved to it before shrivelling to nothing in the heat. All his waking hours had yielded to the marauding night. Entire days shrank into a few sweaty hours. The nocturnal torments reverberated through his twenty-two-year-old mind all through the day. His body ached, his balls were knots of dull pain, taut with overuse. His cock, so unbelievably tender from having been so unbelievably hard, did not feel like it belonged to him any more.

And it didn't.

The curtains fretted in the otherwise still air. She had arrived.

The fluorescent tube coughed briefly, spitting darkness, then recovered. Two weeks ago, he had taken to leaving the lights on in the vain hope that this would either weaken her or strengthen him. Now, she liked it this way. It forced him to see his body being used, watch his cock take on the angles she imposed, watch it shiver uncontrollably as it spewed forth the essence she extracted from him with her mouth, her hands, her dead vagina.

Now into the room she came, and at once her presence pressed down on him. He sank into the sheets, paralysed. His eyes reeled, compensating for his body's immobility, and in answer to his search, she took form. Out of the still air, a faint haze became a fog, then developed outlines and contours, grew solid and opaque ... and then she was there.

She was beautiful, but not in a way the living or sane could possibly comprehend. *What did that make him?* he wondered— but the thought flickered away, terrified of itself.

She, too, was naked—but while his body shuddered with shame, hers was defiantly bared. Her skin shone faintly with a glow that made him think of shapeless, writhing plant-things, fathoms deep in the sea. She must have been young when she died and took this form—how long ago? Decades? Centuries? Living death had drained her of moist youth and left her skin smooth but powdery, her breasts paler and colder than marble.

Her eyes were cruel and colourless. She rarely looked at his face or met his gaze—her obsession lay elsewhere, her control already complete. Her hair glistened but was not wet; moving in response to winds he could not feel. Her teeth were not sharp— she had bitten him often, yet he had never bled—still, they were a predator's teeth. She never touched his lips or kissed him, those actions meant nothing when she could bite, suck, swallow every other inch of him.

She was now stretched out in the air above him, looking ravenously at his meticulously gym-toned body. The inches between them filled with lead, crushing him against the mattress.

Her hands reached down and began to touch him.

Her fingers, cold and raking, ranged across his torso. In the beginning, he had expected to be repulsed by the touch of death, to seek refuge behind stubborn flaccidity. Let her mangle his limp body till she shrieked her way back into the night in banshee frustration, he'd defiantly thought.

But his body was a traitor. While his mind recoiled, scrabbling away from all that she was and everything she did, his body responded to that ancient pact of flesh and lust. Even now, he shuddered and trembled at her touch; as his nipples tingled beneath her fingertips, humiliation rushed to his hot cheeks. He was more disgusted by his own raging flesh than by the outrage of her hands.

Her hands traveled downward, hard nails scraping faint red trails across his helpless abs. And still downward.

His humiliation was now complete. Even before he felt her touch on his cock, he had felt her desire; and already his cock strained towards her, mocking him. Was this the erection dead men had? The hardness of impassive death rather than vigorous life? Was it dead blood that was hardening in his veins, engorging his betrayed manhood?

Then she took him into her mouth, so deep that she would

have choked if she could still breathe. With horror, he felt her lips touch his pubes, his cockhead rub against the flaking inside of her dust-dry throat. The only wetness was his—the shameful ooze of precum that his cock treasonously offered up to lubricate her impalement.

Would she drink his first load? She sometimes did, as if receiving a preliminary offering before the cruel consummation. She could afford to let a load or two go astray, as she seldom left him before he had surrendered his young seed three or four times. In the early weeks, he had felt as if she would empty his balls for good and leave him desiccated , but his body stunned him by repeatedly and consistently satisfying her hunger, against his will.

But this night, her hunger was acute, she wanted his warmth inside her. Already now she was poised over him, her body gaping over his turgid cock. Her eyes met his suddenly, pinning his frantic gaze, and her lips stretched into a merciless leer as she lowered herself onto him. Her cold clamminess drew him in, the emptiness of her pulling him deeper and deeper, as if she would suck his whole body into her—to fill her hollowness, to warm her from the core to the underside of her skin. As if his hot wet life could quench the death that raged in her.

She began riding him, taking him deep with every downward thrust, her body never touching the bed. He could feel the dryness of her vaginal passage rasping against his swollen, throbbing cock. Her silence terrified him: her body displayed all the abandon of lust, but she emitted none of the noisy breathing that underscored physical pleasure. The silence seemed to sharpen her intent, to take all of him, to rape his body until he lost his mind and she possessed his soul.

His young body was stiff against the bed—arms useless, legs unresponsive. He could not resist, could not pull back his groin to deny her. Locked into place, his erection was like a skewed tombstone upon which her insatiable lust perched.

He was getting close. Soon he would offer up this night's first hot libation, a fluid guarantee of his enslaved virility. Any minute now, the dead muscles would gulp at him as his life spurted out in creamy ropes, flowing upwards into whatever emptiness comprised her insides.

As she dragged him towards climax, he understood with searing clarity that he would never belong to anyone else again. Least of all himself. Before anyone else had had the chance, her touch had claimed him. What remained of his life would be spent in the burning shame of nightly surrender ... until he had nothing left to offer, even to her.

And then?

Somewhere inside his head, plummeting downwards through the chasm that her lust had opened in his mind, his dwindling reason began to scream.

And then he came.

Naked Screw

Alison Lester

My apartment in Singapore is immaculate. All the walls are clean and white, except for the one with the naked screw sticking out of it, where I took the wedding photo down. I'm the one who took the picture down; I know what that screw is doing there. But every day it catches my eye, and my brain needs to reassure itself again that the aberration on the wall isn't a threat, a spider or a cockroach, a thing-that-shouldn't-be-there. The broad windows sparkle, the pale grey-and-white marble floor shines so well it reflects perfect rectangles of sky. Now and then, the Singapore Air Force flies its planes overhead, and the reflection of the tiny fighters mimics running cockroaches so well I always speed over to see if I need to stamp on them, just in case.

Once, the shouldn't-be-there thing was bigger. Much bigger.

I'd had my swim and my shower, and was making my usual undressed trip from my bedroom to my kitchen for some juice and yoghurt. I enjoy the cold marble on my feet and the hot sun on my belly and butt as I move through the room. I like to air-dry.

I'd forgotten the building was being painted. Three dark men, South Indians or maybe Bangladeshis, were standing on a suspended platform, staring at me through my living room window. I stopped to think: go to kitchen for food but get stuck there until they descend to paint the lower floors? Or retreat to bedroom and return clothed but still naked in their eyes?

I turned and retreated, but I'd had a good look at them in my moment of indecision. One was so shocked his heavy lower lip hung open, practically flapping in the breeze. One looked wicked to the core. One stared calmly, apparently unruffled, with something just a little fierce around the eyes. As I walked back into the bedroom I felt a strange urge to let these three chocolate men in through the window, into the refrigerated air of my home, so that they wouldn't melt.

I dressed in a khaki skirt and T-shirt and crossed the living room again, aware of the men's shapes suspended behind the couch but not looking at them. Once in the kitchen, I fought the urge to close the door, since I couldn't stay there forever. The alternative was to close the living room curtains. I spooned out my yoghurt and poured my juice, left the kitchen to put them on the dining table, and crossed the living room to the window. I went to the corner where the curtain begins and pulled it across. When I arrived in front of the painters though, I had to stop.

I'd never come this close to a foreign labourer before, window or no window. I'd bought vegetables and ginger from shopkeepers in Little India, but those Indians weren't new to Singapore, or temporary. My gas man is a Chinese Singaporean named Jacky Chan, who complains of having no girlfriends while the movie star has so many. My plumber is a Malay Singaporean named Rosli, who prays in the mosque near my apartment and appears to have no idea that his ring tone is actually the tune to Hava Negila.

I pass foreign labourers in the car and glimpse them digging roadside ditches or pruning the magnificent fecund trees that divide Singapore's expressways. In the evening rush hour, I see them being returned to their sleeping quarters in the backs of open trucks, even when it rains. They have the richest, silkiest hair in the country, and the best hairstyles. They have the roundest muscles. They trump the bespectacled locals for sex appeal. But we don't meet, and we don't talk.

They were so funny, this trio of strangers with paintbrushes. They were working on the stretch of stone under the window, so I could see them from their shoulders up, and their heads were roughly level with my breasts. That's where Mr Flappy Mouth was looking. The devil in the middle was talking, smiling, flashing his white teeth, gesticulating; I understood he was trying to convince me not to close the curtain. The third worker continued to consider me calmly. Even when I looked him straight in the eye.

He's the one who came to the door at lunchtime.

He didn't take off his shoes and make 'may-I-come in?' motions. He stood and stared at me again.

"Hello," I said.

"You offend me," he said. "I am a married man."

"What? It's *my* apartment."

"Cover yourself," he said.

"I *am* covered."

"Cover yourself all day," he said. "Every day. Everywhere." Then he turned to walk back to the elevator. Turning around released the body odour from his clothes. He stank so badly it made my nose itch. It wasn't a street-person stink; it was stewed spices and garlic oozing through his skin on waves of sweat. It touched me that he held his head so high while smelling like he was fermenting.

"Wait a minute," I demanded, wanting revenge.

He turned.

"Was your marriage arranged?"

He nodded.

"Were you allowed to see your wife before you married her?"

"No."

"Wouldn't it have been nice to see her through a window first?"

His head started back as if I had thrust something at him—a snake, or a burning torch—and he turned the corner.

As I prepared my seminar outline that afternoon—I give a kick-ass workshop entitled "PowerPoint Perfection"—I kept thinking about the guys at the window. They live so far from their families if they are married and from potential partners if they are not. I just assumed that they were constantly randy. You can easily get that impression from their curly eyelashes and proud noses. They look imperious, ready to command a woman's favour, even as they inhabit the lowest of the lower echelons of Singapore's workers.

I never expected to be anything less than desired, particularly by guys from the sub-continent. Hindi movies make it clear that they're not afraid of the bigger girl. And now here's this guy telling me I've got it wrong. All afternoon, as I was getting the timing right on the section of my presentation entitled 'Understanding the Human Attention Span', I was thinking this guy must, from time to time, let his mind travel beyond the shores of his wife's body. But I made myself drop the subject when it started feeling like that clichéd argument you listen to at every third or fourth cocktail party in Singapore, the one about the superiority of arranged marriages or love marriages. Not only are these discussions boring, but I'm divorced so I've got no leg to stand on in either camp.

I didn't plan to pursue the subject, with myself or anyone else, but in the early afternoon of the next day, I was walking back to my building from the parking lot when I passed the trio from my window napping on newspapers on the grass by the entrance. Well, the other two were napping. The offended one had his eyes open, and I stopped and looked down into them. I wondered if he'd been thinking about me.

"Why are you not married?" he asked after a moment.

I thought about it. "I'm too tall," I told him.

He laughed. He actually guffawed. The wicked one's eyes rolled a little, but he didn't wake up. Mr Flappy kept on drooling into the sports section.

"Aren't you lonely?" he asked. His consonants sounded as if he were bouncing them off rubber.

"Not really. Aren't you?"

His face clouded over, and he looked away.

"Maybe you have pictures of your wife with you."

He shook his head slightly.

"What about of other women?"

"Stop," he said, and turned onto his side, facing away from me. Like my husband used to, at the end of a bad day.

I went inside. I hadn't swum that morning because I'd been in meetings, pitching my workshop, so I hurried back downstairs in my Speedo, testing myself to see whether walking past him in a swimsuit and towel would make me feel ashamed.

He wasn't there, which made me angry. I did twice as many laps as usual, took a bath, and had a cup of tea standing naked at the living room window.

Once I'd calmed down, though, I was ready to let it go again. He and the boys moved on to Block D, I shot up to Hong Kong to deliver my two-day intensive seminar to the sales team of a major clothing manufacturer, our paths didn't cross. Then, when I got back, I saw him, coming out of the men's toilet by the pool as I was approaching to do laps. When he saw me, he looked like he wanted to turn around, but pulled himself together. We walked toward each other and stopped.

"Hello," I said. I had wanted to sound a bit cold, but it came out warm. I was happy to see him.

"Hello."

"Nearly finished with the painting?"

"No. It is ongoing," he said formally.

"That's work, isn't it? It goes on."

"You are not working."

"I do work."

"Sometimes."

"It pays nicely. And I'm only supporting myself."

"You are completely alone."

"With my thoughts."

He nearly smiled. We were quiet for so long that we either had to say goodbye or open a new subject.

"You went to university, didn't you?" I asked.

"Technical college."

"And what did you study?"

"Electricity."

"Uh-huh? So, tell me, when you were studying, did they give you diagrams of electrical connections to help you understand?"

"Of course."

"Pictures of women also help you understand."

If his skin hadn't been so dark, I'm sure I would have seen him colour in anger.

"We were having a nice conversation. Why did you ruin it?"

"We were having a boring conversation," I said. "Think about it. Excuse me."

I went around him and padded over to the pool. As I dove in and started to pull myself through the water, I had to wonder if I shouldn't be a bit more respectful of his culture, a little more gentle with his sensibilities. But a few laps later I concluded that I was really thinking of his wife. I married a prude myself. They need lessons.

I was ready, then, when he appeared at the end of the pool as I approached for a turn. I stopped, and he asked me, looking straight down his nose, "What is it you want?"

I told him without hesitation: "I want to be your sexy photos."

He looked confused.

"Like in a magazine?" I said. "Do you understand what I mean?"

"I understand. I understand," he said. Then he turned and left, pulling at his lip, looking at the ground.

"Wait!" I shouted.

He stopped without looking around.

"More like in a temple. Like in a Tantric temple."

He turned his head to speak to me over his shoulder.

"You know Tantra?"

"I went to an exhibit in a museum. I went twice actually." It was a few seconds before he walked off again.

I was so excited by what I was proposing that I swam for longer than usual again. It wasn't until I got in the elevator to go back home that I felt like the complete idiot I was. The headline behind my eyes read: SUPER-SIZED WHITE WOMAN OFFERS EDUCATION AND INSPIRATION TO INDIAN ELECTRICIAN, under which hung the tag line: *He's studied the Kama Sutra, lets her down lightly.* I was red with horror at myself from forehead to shoulders by the time I closed my apartment door behind me. I should stick to multimedia presentations. I should go back to the States where we're all as full of ourselves as I am.

And then the doorbell rings. This time I'm not at all prepared that it's him; I'm sure I look just like his pal Mr Flappy when I open the door.

"Okay," he says.

"Okay?"

He nods.

A beatific image forms itself in my head, and I know what to do. "Follow me," I tell him, and lead him to the bathroom.

My bathroom is small, but pretty. You enter through narrow double doors and are facing the sink and mirror. Next to the sink is the toilet. If you sit on the toilet, you are facing the shower, which has two walls of tile and two walls of Plexiglas. I ask the painter to wait outside the door until I'm ready, and close the doors behind me.

Once I've stripped off my swimsuit, I brush out my wet hair so that it hangs down my back, and feel the need to adorn myself. I remember the Tantric statues at the Smithsonian—not only for their buxom figures, their hips cocked to rock against their consorts, and their peaceful, joyful eyes—but also for the detail of their accessories. They were garlanded, with strings of beads or flowers which rested on the upper slopes of their breasts and hung around their rounded bellies, below the navel and above the yoni. I've never in my life seen stone breathe so forcefully.

I start putting on my jewellery, all of it. All my rings, all my bracelets, all my necklaces, pearls, Swarovski, gold and silver chains, and a long, green, beaded belt which I tie around my hips, the feel of which excites me more than a hand

105

could right then.

I step into the shower, then tell him he can come in.

The painter sees where I am and comes to stand in front of the toilet, just a few feet from me. I'm a little nervous, but before I turn on the water, I remember what I teach all my clients about delivering their presentation with confidence and commitment. I look him straight in the eye, surprised to see that this is where he is staring at me as well. I hold up my hands so that he will focus on them, then lay them on my neck and glide them down my body, over my breasts and belly, just as I would have if I'd been allowed to touch the museum sculptures I desired so much.

When I turn the water on, I keep it tepid so that the Plexiglas won't steam up and obscure me. The cool water assures that my nipples will stay erect and my breasts rounded. I soap myself luxuriously but naturally, thinking more of my own pleasure than of his, teaching him about women, about women alone. Then I take the showerhead off its hook to rinse myself. I pull my left leg up and press my knee against the wall, opening myself completely for view. For the first time in my life, I'm convinced beyond any doubt that my pussy is something sacred, something to be adored, worthy of sculpture and ceremony.

The painter thinks so as well. He sits on the toilet seat and opens his trousers, untangling his hard-on from his flimsy boxer shorts and letting his cock stand on view, like a statue, like me, before starting to stroke himself. He watches as I move the showerhead all over my head and body. I want to touch myself as well, but I don't. The sculptures don't, so I don't. They just look healthy and contented, so I am too.

The painter's climax is a quiet event. I know that when I experience the pleasure of climax, my face shows pain. Ecstasy as excruciation. But his face remains calm, and his eyes stay on my body.

Whatever he feels when he comes, I certainly feel released from something.

While he cleans himself up, I turn off the shower and stand inside it, the light sparkling on the wet links and crystals, until he is finished. He fastens his trousers again, and stands in front of me with the clear door between us.

"Thank you," he says seriously, just like a student would, and leaves. Once I'm dry and wrapped in my towel, I go out to the living room, but he's gone.

I don't expect to see the painter again, and I don't mind. He turned out to be a should-be-there thing. Like the screw. It's an aberration, but it's useful. I can put up a new picture whenever I want.

Body Drafts

Rachel Loh

After removing her bra, Michelle slowly slipped off her more reluctant panties, then stood there holding both. She looked over at Dr Narain sheepishly, the underwear dangling from her hand.

"Anywhere," Narain said with a generous shrug. "Just throw them over there."

Michelle turned and tossed first the bra, then the panties onto a tawny brown plush chair squeezed next to the bedroom dresser. She then turned back to Dr Narain, arms folded lengthwise across her front, as if to attempting to cover her breasts and crotch—though very little of either was covered.

"It's more comfortable here than in my office, isn't it?" said Dr Narain. "Not as cold, I think." A knowing smile filtered in. "In any sense."

"Yes," Michelle giggled. "It is much more comfortable here. Very much." She laughed again, then let her arms fall to her sides. After all, this was hardly the first time Narain had seen her naked body. The only difference was that this time they were in the doctor's bedroom, not the office. After exchanging conspiratorial smiles with Narain, Michelle folded her arms behind her back, shifted her feet, threw her head back and posed, showing off her work-in-progress body.

Narain beamed, stepped forward and started caressing the edges of that delicate Chinese face, finally streaming skilled fingers through the patient's hair. "Admiring your work?" Michelle asked with a nervous smile.

"Admiring your beauty," Narain replied, with a more confident smile. Michelle closed her eyes and leaned her head back further, allowing Narain to caress her more easily. She did, indeed, feel comfortable in the hands of this doctor. From that very first time she stepped into the office and saw Narain, she felt surprisingly at ease, glad that she had taken her friend Tania's advice and sought out this particular specialist.

Michelle had been going to Dr Narain for just over a year now. She had started with botox treatments, then went on to collagen infusions, before moving up to minor surgery to give her the double eyelid that all affluent Asian women seem required to sport these days. Only recently had she decided to ask Narain about more radical procedures: body sculpting, breast enlargement, vaginal tightening. Though still anxious about this next stage, she was nonetheless determined to press ahead with it.

Narain had moved from stroking Michelle's hair and face and was now skimming the tips of well-trained fingers across the patient's neck. "Yes, you can use a little bit of work here. Don't worry, we'll get these lines gone completely. Very simple. We can do it next week at the office, if you like."

"Botox?" Michelle asked. Narain gave another generous,

reassuring smile, along with a shake of the head. "No, that won't work here. What we're looking at is just a short deep laser treatment. Fifteen minutes, tops, for this lovely neck of yours. And no down time really."

Michelle nodded, just as Narain started grazing fingers lightly over her shoulders, before slowly easing them down to the outer curve of her breasts. Michelle again closed her eyes and took long, deep breaths.

"I think your breasts are just ... wonderful," Narain told her. "They are *so* right for you. Why so many women here want those big, lumpy Western appendages, like the things poor Pamela Anderson has to struggle around with, I just don't understand. It's terrible."

"Yes, I agree, Doctor. But my husband says they're too small—especially for the wife of someone in his position. He'd like something a little closer to Pamela's problem." During this exchange, Narain's hands had cupped Michelle's petite breasts and were now fondling them gently, working the palms dexterously along the soft, pliant curves.

"Well then, whatever ... But like I've told you already, I think your husband is an absolute idiot." For emphasis on this point, Narain started fondling the breasts with vigour. Michelle breathed deeply, bit her lower lip, then whispered out her reply.

"You are absolutely right. He is an idiot, A-list idiot actually, but he pays all the bills. Including all your bills."

"For which, I am eternally grateful," Narain answered, then leaned over and placed an eager mouth to Michelle's nipples.

First, the doctor's lips gently grazed against the broad aureole and nipples, already hardened, before an ardent tongue started flicking against them. Soon, lips and tongue both began sucking in soft, measured pulls, as Michelle eagerly lost control.

She started running her hands wildly through the dark tangles of Narain's hair, then, as Narain nuzzled upwards and started planting deep kisses on the neck, she dropped her hands to the doctor's hips and rubbed vigorously, before gliding the hands around to clutch Narain's well-toned butt. Narain responded instantly: the doctor's crotch was pressed tightly against Michelle's. As Narain took Michelle's face and the two kissed fully on the mouth, their loins started grinding rhythmically against each other. Then, as the tongues lashed in slow swirls upon each other, the twists of the loins grew longer, slower, more charged with purpose.

When they broke to seize a few breaths, Michelle gave a light push and stepped back. "Maybe we'd better change tactics here, or you're going to have to rush those pants of yours right over to the dry-cleaners. And I have no idea how easy it is to get out those kinds of spots."

Narain again flashed that soft, reassuring smile. "To hell with it: I'll just keep them as a souvenir of a very wonderful time in my life." As Michelle grinned shyly, Narain leaned over and planted a quick, affectionate kiss on her lips. "But you're right; it is unfair that I'm always 'in uniform' while you're in various stages of undress." The doctor then turned and indicated the bed with a theatrical flourish of the hand. "Anyway, it's time we moved on to the next phase of the examination. So ... shall we move to the ... examination table, Mrs Tay?"

With an enthusiastic nod, Michelle padded over to the bed. Narain, already barefoot, followed just behind.

"Oh, I really like this examination table," Michelle said, climbing onto the bed and sitting up, as her shapely legs (no work needed there) slid back and forth along the length of the bed. "Especially the 40-thread cotton sheets you've got on it." Narain nodded. "Much better than those cold, metal stirrups in your office."

"All in the interests of making the patient more comfortable, of course," Narain said, starting to undo those pants Michelle had been so concerned about.

"Of course," Michelle echoed, watching captivated as the doctor shed the other articles of clothing. Within moments, all of Narain's clothing had been dropped to the floor, and the doctor spread both arms out like wings, showing off that very enviable body.

Although they'd had sort-of-sex several times in the surgery office, Michelle had never before seen Narain completely naked. She now found herself thoroughly aroused by the doctor's well-sculpted form.

"God, you've got a great body there." She smiled impishly, like a schoolgirl having happened upon an adult's locked-up secret. "Did you go under the knife yourself to get there? Or get lasered, or whatever you can do these days?"

"That, my dear, is a professional secret. It would be a gross violation of the plastic surgeon's code to reveal such details about a patient—any patient."

113

Michelle laughed. "And isn't it maybe a teensy, weensy violation of the surgeon's code to have sex with a patient—one still undergoing treatment?"

"Hmm," replied Narain, "Now that you mention it, I think there is something about that in the code. But we don't want to violate too many parts of the code all at once now, do we?"

Narain had by this point shuffled to the edge of the bed. Reaching down with the skill, tact and delicacy of a doctor starting a probe, Narain took Michelle's right foot, raised it about six inches, then—while staring right into her eyes—started stroking the sole. "Now, what about these? Is your husband satisfied with your feet?" Narain started running two deft fingers along the easy curve of the foot. "Sure he doesn't want the arches raised a little, perhaps lowered a little?"

"No, I think he's fine with the feet," Michelle answered, as her eyelids slid closed in enjoyment of this impromptu massage.

"Oh really? So he doesn't want me to add a few dimples to the toes? Make them even more delectable?" At this, the doctor raised Michelle's foot slightly higher and started sucking on those toes. This sent Michelle into a slow spin of ecstasy, which only intensified as Narain turned the foot gently and started slowly licking the sole. The doctors' tongue flowed along the pinkish skin, paused to give one spot special treatment, flowed again. In muted rapture, Michelle herself raised the other foot and rubbed it against the doctor, from the strong chin down to just below the waist.

Narain put the two feet together, kissed each one, then slowly lowered them back onto the bed. Michelle looked up with keen anticipation. When Narain answered this look with a feigned quizzical expression, Michelle reached for the doctor. Smiling, Narain took her hand, caressed it, then slipped fully onto the bed, next to her. With head raised, supported by the left arm, the doctor gave a slow, appreciative scrutiny along the entire length of her body. It was clear that Narain took both pride and delight in attending to Michelle and all her needs.

"So, Doctor, do you think there's hope for me?"

"Oh … much hope; much, much hope," the surgeon replied, allowing a hand to roll slowly over the slope of Michelle's thighs. "It's just a matter of determining what we want and then, you know, setting out the proper body drafts."

"Body drafts?" Michelle was obviously amused by the term.

"Yes, my darling—body drafts. We examine the basic material, sketch out a working topography, then decide what we wish to create out of that. The actual surgery is the hard part, of course; taking body drafts is much easier and, I have to say, *much* more fulfilling." At this, Narain leaned over as if to kiss her, but suddenly stopped short and delivered a playful tickle instead.

Michelle, of course, laughed and in the middle of her laughter managed to say, "Alright, Doctor, let's see how you carry out your drafts." She pointed a mock warning finger at the beaming face. "And I expect a thorough job here."

"Of course; you should expect nothing less from me. Let's see: we can easily sculpt a more svelte curvature here …" the doctor's hand slid up the thigh, all the way to the place where it met the other, lingering there a few moments "... and here." Narain now began squeezing the hips, which Michelle had long considered too well padded.

"And there's no problem at all shaping this luscious part." Narain had just swung one leg over the patient and was now straddling Michelle as the trained surgeon's hands did a quick draft of the buttocks, kneading the soft flesh as if about to sculpt it into a splendidly taut masterwork. Michelle elevated her hips slightly, allowing the doctor's strong fingers to slip in and then run along the crack of the ass from top to bottom. The fingers gently rotated as they made their way down the soft cleft. Like that first time it had happened at the office, Michelle was amazed at how much pleasure she could take from this 'disgusting' manoeuvre—when done by someone who obviously knew what they were doing.

Still arched over Michelle's eager body, supported by elbows and knees, Narain bent down until moistened lips hovered maybe an inch away from the breasts. "And there are just... so many possibilities with these beauties here." The tongue, the teeth, the lips now swept all over Michelle's breasts, sending the patient into deeper ecstasy.

"And as for that vaginal tightening your idiot husband wants ..."

"Yes, Doctor, yes-s-s?"

"Well, let's explore the territory in question."

As Narain said this, two skilled fingers were already slipping inside Michelle, testing pleasure spots Michelle herself had somehow always neglected until Narain had taught her a month and a half ago. The very willing patient rose slightly and began swivelling on these two fingers as Narain, now repositioned, eased the same two fingers from the other hand in and began rotating vigorously in close rhythm to Michelle's gyrations.

Her eyes shut tightly, fingers squeezed into Narain's shoulders, Michelle thrust herself on and around the fingers until, within maybe twenty seconds, she came. Then, clutching the doctor's wrists, she pushed down, intensifying the pleasure as she swelled into a second orgasm. Oh God, I always come with Dr Narain, she thought—even those crazy times in the office, where it was so cold and rushed, with a pack of other patients waiting impatiently outside.

Always came. She told herself it was simply because Narain was a doctor, a surgeon trained in handling those most intricate— and intimate—parts of the body that she could … She didn't dare to try on any other explanation for Narain's unfailing success at bringing her to orgasm. After another few moments, Michelle opened her eyes and peered with a swirl of love-lust at this highly skilled healer.

"And your husband wants this lovely passage tightened?" The doctor's brow furrowed in mock bewilderment. "I don't know. It certainly works for *me*." The fingers started churning around again energetically. "And most important, Michelle darling, it clearly works for you. Oh yes: definitely." The fingers still there inside the patient, Narain bent over to kiss Michelle gently on the lips. As their lips brushed against each other,

117

Michelle grabbed the back of the doctor's head, pulled it in closer and turned that gentle kiss into a long, urgent, passionate embrace.

At the end of the kiss, Narain rose off Michelle slightly, pulling the fingers back until just the tips were still inside. As those tips started rotating gently, Michelle was filled with a fierce urge to give the doctor as much pleasure as she had just taken, more if possible ... yes, more and more—for both of them. More.

In high arousal, she pulled herself up slightly and reached out—reached out to take Dr Narain's breasts, pulling at those gorgeous tits, much larger than her own, then rose and, while still massaging the breasts, started sucking desperately at one dark nipple, then the other. As she sucked, she also moved her left hand to the doctor's own vagina and started stroking along the moist slit, caressing its cushion of tightly whorled hair.

As Michelle pulled back to see the mounting rapture on her physician's face, she managed to push this larger woman down on her back and whispered, "So, Dr Narain, do you like the taste of your own medicine?"

The doctor put her hand over Michelle's and started pressing hard against it. "Oh yes, yes indeed. I think I'd even enjoy a little overdose, if you don't mind."

By now, Michelle had slipped her own fingers into Narain. She bowed lower and before starting to trace her tongue along the sweet curve of the doctor's lovely left breast, she replied, "Well, we'll give it all we can. But you'll have to tell me if I'm doing everything right. After all, you're the doctor, Dr Narain."

"Please," she murmured, "call me Vivien."

Michelle looked up from the robust mound of the doctor's breasts. "Alright then ... Vivien. You know, Vivien, I'm beginning to see just what you mean about the fun of taking body drafts."

An MRT Chronicle

Weston Sun Wensheng

The girl had dozed off, clutching her handbag and a large manila envelope to her chest. Her long hair covered most of her face. He was waiting, and hoping.

He found his seat and was looking forward to a nap on the train ride home. He had left the office late. It was almost eleven and the train was not crowded. There were many empty seats. He changed his mind about the nap when he saw her.

Seated right across him, he had not noticed her at first. She was another office girl. Her slim frame was clad in a white blouse, grey skirt and stilettos. Pretty in a common way. Like one of the many office girls one sees on the train. She had long, straightened hair with brownish streaks and smooth, fair skin. Nothing special. Another one off the production line from Singapore Inc., Model: Office Girl, Design A32.

She sat slumped over, unperturbed by the lunatic beeps that warned of closing train doors. He would not have observed her so carefully if not for the fact that in her exhausted slumber, her legs were threatening to spread open right before him.

The frontal slit in her skirt had offered him a glimpse of naked, smooth flesh. He could see from the slightly parted legs that the girl had slim, firm thighs. As she had shifted in her sleep, her skirt had bunched up and the slit had moved up. He could see even further up her thighs. "Just a little higher," he thought, while he made sure to pick up his briefcase from the floor and put it over his crotch.

From the corner of his eye, he noticed that a plump, oily-looking Chinese man was also staring in the direction of the office girl's parted legs. But he had a better view than Oily Man. He had been lucky enough to choose the seat directly across from the office girl.

With a gentle cough, the office girl slid further down her seat while still clutching tightly to her handbag and envelope. After what seemed like an eternity of waiting, she spread her legs wide open. At this, it seemed like Oily Man stopped breathing.

He had a clear view of her panties. They were a thin white material that stretched tightly across her fleshy mound. Her neat, dark patch showed through the white translucency. He felt the urge to finger the girl's pussy. He imagined it would be slippery and soft. He felt the blood race to his cock.

Home was an "executive apartment" in government housing parlance. He lived with his parents and older sister at the top of the government-housing totem pole. A spacious, air-conditioned apartment with marble and wood flooring, it was comfortable and just a seven-minute walk from the train station, the transportation lifeline of himself and many of his countrymen. Like long-ago villagers who congratulated themselves on their good fortune if they could build a home near a water source, he and his family had felt fortune smiling upon them when they received the news from the government agency that they would get a flat near the MRT train station.

His mother asked the usual questions as he arrived home. "Ah Boy, are you hungry?" "Ah Boy, would you like to eat now?" "Ah Boy, how was work today? Ah Boy was his childhood nickname, one he shared with every other Chinese male under thirty in Singapore. He gave the usual replies: "No, I'm not hungry, but I will eat a little." "Very busy at work today."

He remembered his mother's latest ailment and dutifully asked if her cough was better. As usual, she said it was not, that it had gotten worse. Her current ailment generally worsened until a replacement ailment came along. He told her to take care of herself, said something nice about the meal and excused himself with the usual platitudes: he was tired and had work to do in his room. He left to take his shower, leaving his mother to her Chinese drama serials.

He ejaculated quickly and showered. Thoughts of the office girl's open legs and a popular local actress were meshed into one grand threesome fantasy of transparent white panties, long dark hair, and pale smooth skin.

Meanwhile, he looked forward to the next day, watching soccer over a few beers with Terence.

Trains headed towards the city were usually crowded that time of the day during weekends, but the train delay announcement usually meant that trains would be sardine-packed. He didn't get a seat, but found a spot that allowed his back to rest against a plastic partition, largely taken as a decent consolation prize amongst Singapore train travellers.

The train was jammed with bodies due to the delay. He tried not to have any part of his body touch or be touched by the sweaty construction worker who stood facing him. He could smell the worker's foul breath and sweat. He hoped the train would not jerk and throw the man against him or the other way round. But good fortune smiled upon him: the construction worker got off at the next stop.

Taking the foul-smelling construction worker's place was a teenage girl who was heavily perfumed and made up. She was one of those social profiles government leaders and elders in the community fretted over. If one could judge a book by its cover, she looked quite capable of committing all the sins the community assiduously guarded against: drugs, teenage pregnancy, dropping out of school.

The girl had smooth, lightly tanned skin, a sweet face and a body that, though slightly plump, curved in all the right places. Standing very close to him and facing him, she reached up to his neck.

She wore a tiny spaghetti-strapped top that clearly showed a soft, fleshy cleavage. Her blouse was cut low. He estimated he was just an inch or so from seeing nipples. More people came on board. The girl's body now pressed against his. Thankfully, he had on a pair of Levis that could contain his bulge. She looked up at him and proffered a shy half-smile. He responded with a look of seeming discomfort. She let out a startled girlish cry as the train jerked and her body was pushed closer to his. Her breasts were now squeezed hard against his middle torso while his groin was squashed against her body. Another shy half-smile; she didn't seem to mind the pressing. It was almost like no-motion copulation, with clothes on, in public. He liked the closeness, though he continued to display a look of irritation. The no-motion copulation soon stopped. It was Bugis station and many people streamed out into the popular shopping spot. She got off at the next stop. The pretend sex made him a little tired. He needed a beer badly.

"And she wanted to go to the backseat right, so I said okay lor, then she just sat in front of me, took my cock, put on the condom for me, stick my cock inside her *chee bai* and started fucking me. You believe it or not! She fucked me! I didn't have to do any work at all. And she was so wet, I was afraid she'll drip on the leather and I have no idea what that kind of erm … water, no not water … liquid, ya that kind of liquid does to leather, whether the stain was removable, you know. I told you I had the maintenance done only recently, and it's calf leather, right, so, of course, I was bit worried …" It was the soccer break and Terence was regaling him with a story of another one-night stand with a disco pickup. Listening to Terence talk, he never ceased to marvel at how Terence had been virtually untainted by his stint in America.

Terence had it all—except looks, academic ability and charm. So, he didn't have it all, but his family had money. Terence's lack of many gifts didn't seem to stop the women. Ah Boy was the one who had to slog it out in secondary school for the very competitive admissions to a top local junior college while Terence smoked, expended time and energy hiding cigarette packs from school prefects, and dated a very busty junior college girl who had a reputation for being wild. Terence proceeded to fail his government exams in grand fashion, then his parents predictably put up a princely sum for his National Service bond and bought him, with another princely sum, a place at an American university where history repeated itself—he did not study, he smoked and he had lots of sex. The two men weren't exactly, as the saying goes, peas in the pod, but they had played and watched soccer together for way too long and had acquired the status of longtime friends.

Terence Tan Chwee Beng was blessed with some humility though. "Of course, with a car like that, it's easy to find girls to screw." Ah Boy didn't have a BMW Coupe and could not afford one in a country where such a vehicle cost more than a quarter of a million dollars. The family Nissan Sunny plastered with religious slogans on the windscreens did not work the same magic with women.

He had been thinking of buying a car of his own. The family Nissan wasn't always available and even when it was, he had always felt at least a tad guilty getting a blow job in the car. His parents had been zealous in expressing their religiosity through the vehicle. The car had been plastered with decals bearing slogans encouraging the faithful to be more faithful and the unconverted to convert.

It was not easy to decide though. There was a quota for the

number of cars allowed in the tiny island-state. And one had to bid for the right to own one. He had been monitoring the COE (Certificate of Entitlement), prices for the under-1.6-litre category. With a COE, a Mitsubishi Lancer should set him back by S$52,000.

There were few venue options for unmarried couples to get hot and steamy on this hot and steamy little island. Hotels required the identity card numbers of their guests, and, like many of his peers, he was too shy to be seen checking into one in his home country and a few privately felt that these visits might be recorded in some secret government file. Subsidised government housing was for married couples and unsubsidised housing was beyond the reach of many, including himself. In any case, like many of his peers, he would not wish to hurt his mother's feelings by moving out before he got married. He could bring a girl home while his folks went on holiday, but that was once a year. He could always leave the country with a girl to fuck. A holiday was a good cover. But that would be twice a year at best.

The car was one option, though it had its limitations. He would not fuck in the family car. Some petting and head was okay, but no fucking. What if the police arrived while he was in the middle of it or while he came? And those slogans.

"Hey, you got yourself some fun or not?" Terence, remembering his manners, enquired.

"No time. Some people have to work you know," he replied good-naturedly. Which was partially true. He did work and was sensibly striving to save so he could invest his savings wisely or maybe buy a car.

In the meantime, he was satisfied with the very efficient and clean MRT system. It had served him well as a means of transport and S$52,000, not including road tax and gasoline, was not a small sum of money. At the same time, he wanted the independence and flexibility of owning his own vehicle, then he could always park somewhere dark with a girl and they could do what they wanted. With someone such as Ling, for instance.

He had gotten to know Ling not from any religious organization or activity, as was his usual practice, but from an Internet dating site. She was not quite his usual type. And except that he was tall with a pleasing face, neither was he her type. He was attracted to, yet afraid of, what he had considered her wildness and he had lied to her about where he worked and where he lived. She was a startling orange spot in a sea of pastels. Ling laughed loudly, wore bright red lipstick and had blonde streaks in her long, curly black hair. Unlike his previous girlfriends, who were slim with small breasts, Ling had large breasts and a big ass. And unlike his previous girlfriends who were martyrs when it came to sex, Ling had said to him without shame, "I love sex."

On their second date, he had driven her to a dark spot near the Botanical Gardens in his parents' Sunny. They had gone to the back seat after he parked. She lost no time in pulling down her flimsy top to reveal a transparent bra. Even in the darkness, her large, erect nipples could be clearly seen through the bra. Her strong perfume and her moans had also excited him. He squeezed her breasts and bent down to lick and suck her nipples one at a time. When the material was soaked, she eagerly pulled her bra down so that he might enjoy her in the flesh.

"I want to suck cock," she moaned. And before he could react, she had unzipped his pants and proceeded to lick his penis slowly and then, inch by inch, took all six inches in her mouth like a circus sword swallower. He could hardly bear it. With her bright red lipstick staining his penis and the fingers of one hand pinching her left nipple and the other hand squeezing her right breast, he wanted to ejaculate into her mouth.

"Fuck me, please. I beg you to fuck me," Ling murmured.

He had been so absorbed in playing those large, soft breasts that were such an exhilarating novelty to him, and taking in the view of her thick red lips on his penis, that he had forgotten to feel up her pussy. On the word "fuck," he lost no time in pulling up her pink miniskirt. She was wearing a pair of light-colored net panties that clearly showed a large untamed patch of pubic hair. He stuck one finger in. Her hole was hot and sticky, and her juices had dripped to her inner thighs. She moaned.

"Stick your hard cock in, please."

He made a quick mental calculation. There was only a fifty-fifty chance of the police coming round. And Ling, all tits and ass, was a dream fuck. She had even brought along her own condoms. So he thought he should. Then, in the midst of preparing for entry, he spotted part of one of his parents' decals: "Yield not to Temptation." And he could not fornicate.

"Just suck me," he said.

"Why?" she shot back quickly.

"You'll do it so well, that's why," he responded in a tone

that attempted to pacify.

"I want you to fuck me. If you're not going to fuck me, I'm not going to suck anymore," she stated firmly. Then, after some negotiation, they masturbated each other to orgasm. But she didn't answer his calls and text messages after that evening.

He wanted his own car, a car without slogans. He would have fucked her until he hurt himself, if not for that slogan.

It was the last train home. The next game was between some second-tier teams. He had one more beer with Terence. "Best to leave early," he thought; so he skipped the last game and caught the train to save on cab fare.

Another last train home.

As usual, passengers gradually filtered out of the train as it went further out towards his destination, the last station of the line. Exhausted, he looked unthinkingly around him. Further along the train, on the row of seats diagonally opposite to his, sat a young couple, clearly impatient for some physical action and not much caring for waiting any longer.

They were sitting side by side but their bodies were turned, twisted almost, towards each other. He had his left arm around her shoulders, his right hand on her thighs, his head was bent forward, his mouth covering hers, and the way he pushed against her face almost looked like the kissing would break her neck. His right hand strayed lower on her thighs, towards her knees and slipped under her short skirt, lifting the hem slightly until he could reach where the thighs met. She lifted her eyes while still kissing him, reached for her jacket and pulled it over their thighs, then opened her legs wider. Ah Boy was sitting quite a length away but from his angle, he could get a good look at exactly what the couple was doing.

She was getting more active in her participation. From the lifting and sinking of the jacket, it was obvious she was doing something with her hands to his crotch. After a few minutes more of this suggestive but hidden action under the jacket, she pulled away from kissing him, leaned forward and actually put her head under the jacket.

As the guy leaned back against the seat, head resting on the window behind him, arms spread out on both sides to rest on the top of the seats, the jacket began dancing slowly. Up and down in a steady motion. A contented smile spread across the guy's face as he closed his eyes, savouring the attention given to him under cover.

The guy opened his eyes and looked in Ah Boy's direction. Their eyes met. Ah Boy averted his eyes quickly but just as quickly brought them back to the irresistible show. The guy smiled smugly.

He thought it surreal that he should be looking at the couple in their intimacy and in a very public environment but he didn't dwell on the thought and kept looking. He wanted to watch as one would want to watch a pornographic video. The young couple didn't seem to care either and he wasn't committing any crime looking at them. Ah Boy licked his lips, and pondered as he watched and his cock throbbed. "Are there cameras in here? Is the driver monitoring this and recording it?" He looked around and didn't see any cameras.

He felt a movement near him but his eyes continued to be glued to the show, to the dancing jacket of his fellow passenger. The destination announcement came and, following some frantic fumbling with their clothing, the couple got off the train.

Why did this keep happening to him and yet not happening to him? He was always the audience of someone else's show, the spectator to another hero's triumph, always close enough to smell the blood but kept just at an arm's length away from tasting it.

"That was nice wasn't it?" a low female voice startled him. It was Ling who had slipped into the seat next to him. With his intense concentration on the dancing jacket, he had not noticed her when she sat quietly down next to him.

He got over his surprise at the coincidental meeting quickly and instinctively he replied, "Aiyoh, how could people do that here, tsk?"

"Why not?" Ling said, as she let her hand rest on his thigh. "Let me show you how she did it and I could also show you more. Much, much more," Ling's breath got heavier as she took off her jacket and put it over his lap.

"Just relax," she said. And he obeyed.

He couldn't believe his ears. The audience had just been invited onto the stage.

A Dummy's Guide
To Losing Your Virginity

Meihan Boey

> "Shall I tell you what makes love so dangerous?
> T'is the too high idea we are apt to form of it."
> —Ninon L'Enclos, 17th-century courtesan

I lost my virginity to a man named Pierre two weeks after meeting him.

Well, *of course*, Pierre isn't his real name. How many real Frenchmen do you know named Pierre? Enid Blyton names every other Frenchman "Pierre" in her kiddie novels, but in real life, most Frenchmen have names like Philippe or Jean or something entirely unpronounceable. It's never as simple as Pierre.

Anyway, Pierre isn't French, he's Belgian. He is whiter than white, has perfect skin (perfect enough, that is, to be remarkable for his age), brown eyes, sandy-grey hair, and a huge cock that swells up and sticks out perpendicularly from his very thin body like a rose-red battering ram.

I was saying that I lost my virginity to him two weeks after meeting him. I suppose you're wanting an explanation of this somewhat extraordinary statement. It's just not worth the bother. Therefore, feel free to fit us both into any convenient category of human behaviour. Rest assured, I will not complain. Complaining, I find, is the refuge of the weak and unimaginative who have neither the courage to put up with shit nor the wherewithal to get out of it.

However I *will* answer the usual round of questions.

1. Yes, he is married.
2. Yes, I knew it.
3. Yes, he's a horny old man. Exactly 23 years older than me, if you like precise figures.
4. Yes, I am Asian—Chinese, if you also enjoy precise descriptions. And I therefore qualify, as my little brother pointed out with a shudder, as an SPG.
5. No, he didn't dump me after one night of sex ... BUT!
6. Yes, the relationship is pretty much all about sex.

By the way, yes, you are free to join my brother and think of me as an SPG. I like the phrase "Sarong Party Girl" really. Wear a sarong, go out and party. Of course, the SPG's reason for wearing a sarong—or whatever conveniently unwrappable dress is in fashion these days—and going to a party is usually to pick up a White Man. Whether or not this was my specific intention while partying in a sarong, I'm not bothering to clarify. You are perfectly free to draw your own conclusions about me, as I am of you.

I became Pierre's mistress without intending to. What I *was* intending was to do was sleep with him so as to get rid of my tiresome virginity, which had been left stubbornly on my hands for 26 years.

I was telling you Pierre had a cock like a battering ram. A virgin pussy becomes deeply startled when faced with the prospect of penetration by a battering ram. A pulse of sheer panic raced up and down me when the whole bulk of it emerged from between the silver teeth of his zipper.

"That's not going to fit! It's HUGE!" I bellowed, flinging all thought of seductive atmosphere, which I'd been carefully building up for three hours, to the winds. Pierre shook his head, disparagingly. "Average," he murmured, "average."

The average size of the male penis is six to seven inches erect. Proportionately, Pierre was not wrong, though, for he is six foot tall. His problem is that he is underweight for his height, so that a penis which would have looked relatively proportionate for a six-foot, 180-pound man, looks preposterously gargantuan for a six-foot man who only weighs 135 pounds.

Now, I am very short, even for an Asian girl. I didn't even know if I had enough piping for this plunger.

"Think of it as a baby's head," he persuaded me silkily, pushing me quite firmly down under him. "That's what it's built for, right?"

"I suppose so," I replied dubiously, and gritted my teeth.

Pierre had been told by a friend that I was a virgin. He did not believe I was a virgin. I did not act like a virgin and I hadn't bothered to tell him. Because if I had, he wouldn't have slept with me; it's that simple.

"I shouldn't have been your first experience," he exclaimed in dismay when he finally asked and I told him.

This surprised me, because I had judged him at first glance very much the way you might have been doing up to this point. I had seen a nattily dressed, charmingly seductive older European man, freely discussing his experiences with many girlfriends. I had therefore fit him neatly into that handy category, the Horny White Man.

Oh, let me elaborate just a little. Horny White Man: Good in bed, generous with women, dislikes long-term relationships, probably divorced/married, adulterous. The HWM is the antithesis of the SPG, which is why they are drawn to each other. HWMs are for the most part weak in character, strong in personality, easily led but difficult to pin down. It takes our strong-willed SPGs five minutes to lead a HWM to the altar, and an ensuing five years (or the equivalent in alcohol) to force them to sign the registry.

I suppose there are degrees of Horny White Man-ness, just as there are degrees of Sarong Party Girl-ness. Some are merciless, some are buoyant with random sincere affection, some are in-between. I am in-between; Pierre, as I grow to know him, is closer to the extreme of sincere, emotional attachment for every beautiful woman on earth, and some not so beautiful as well. (And a few who are not, technically, women. Don't ask.)

But we were talking about the sex.

I believe the secret to good sex is enjoying your own body. I am inordinately vain about my body. I have perfect breasts, each one a nice firm but soft handful, set high and full against my ribcage; I have a splendid waist, nicely tucked-in, and very comfortable, plus round, dimpled arms and legs. I have little love for my ass, but Pierre turned out to like it best, so altogether I believe myself a regular Aphrodite, and knowing oneself to be an Aphrodite does wonders for one's performance in bed.

A book called *The Satanic Witch* suggests that men are most turned on by underwear they're *not* supposed to be seeing (i.e. not the half-naked stripper doing the pole dance on the stage, but the primly dressed girl whose thong might be just peeking out over the top of her jeans). Most importantly, one must make the most of what one has, whether it be sexual charisma, bedroom eyes, or a good set of tits. The important thing is to seem accessible without seeming easy.

I have always loved my tits. The first man to squeeze them was a fellow called Jeff. He watched me dancing on a platform with my tits on the verge of bouncing entirely free of my slightly exposed bra, until he approached me for a dance and took the opportunity to grope me, first one breast, then the other. Growing bolder, he pressed his fingers inside my blouse, then my bra, and fingered my nipples. That was rather nice, but then I decided he would be no fun as a First Experience (random gropers seldom are) and escaped.

On the whole, I am glad I waited for Pierre, who flirted before he seduced, and seduced before he groped, which is only polite.

The first part of me he saw naked was my left breast, which he peeked at by lifting the corner of my blouse. Being very pleased with my breasts, as I've explained, I allowed him.

137

"Now I can't stand up," he murmured, smiling faintly. "Everyone will see."

I thought this rather complimentary, considering the vast number of tits he has seen in his career as a ladies' man. We then progressed, after a great deal of impolite cuddling, to bed.

Having believed myself in possession of a perfect body for so long, it seemed a marvelous moment to finally show it off, in all its glory, for another human being's appreciation. It was unwrapped by stages; it was rubbed first, through my clothes, through my bra, then under my bra, which was finally unhooked. I presented my naked tits to him for further attention, which he gave most obligingly. He then searched under my skirt, discovered perfectly ordinary white cotton panties and was extremely pleased.

This is not to say that I lay there like a blow-up doll. I had saved my virginity not out of a sense of sexual morality, but out of an abhorrence of waste; I didn't want to waste that first, irretrievable experience on the male version of a blow-up doll. I therefore had no intention of being anything less than responsive. Being determined to leave my state of inexperience with a vengeance, I began with what would become my favourite beginning—a blow job.

Blow jobs interest me. I have a friend for whom sex has been a matter-of-fact affair since the age of fourteen. She has made love in all conceivable positions, licked, sucked, tickled and teased every easily accessible orifice of her longtime boyfriend's body (and he hers), attempted interesting experiments with honey, wax, chocolate, whipped cream. Yet her imagination is not what one would call vast.

"What does cock taste like?" I asked her eagerly once.

She shrugged disinterestedly. "Like skin, lah," she replied.

Admittedly, her simple answer made me a whole lot less afraid of giving a blow job, and when I finally had the chance to fit a cock into my mouth, I went at it with enthusiasm. Let it never be said that I give a sloppy blow job! Oh no. The very idea of a blow job deeply entices me.

There is so much to a man's cock besides the taste of skin, lah. There is the thin, silky texture of the shaft as your tongue slides over it, the soft, warm marshmallow of the head that quickly tightens into a hot, quivering ball when your lips close over it. I have longed to give a blow job ever since I read about it in my mother's copy of *Everywoman*, to find all the tickly bits with my tongue and suck milk from the tip like an infant on a nipple. To feel the soft flesh grow hot and stiff in my mouth is an instant of the most irrevocable power a woman can have over a man. In short? Cock, basically, tastes pretty damn good.

Another question I asked my matter-of-fact friend: what does semen taste like?

"Salty," she said.

Another, more descriptive girl said, "At first, it's thick and goes goosh, goosh, goosh. After that it's thinner and kind of watery and it just goes spurt. Splut. Sppt."

I investigated with great interest the taste of semen. This particular batch was, well, salty. With a hint of cigarettes and alcohol. And it was something between the goosh and the splut.

139

Having been a virgin for twenty-six years, I'd had plenty of time to consider what a cock would feel like, as well as taste like. "It's a muscle," Pierre explained to me one day, much later, favouring me also with the various Latinate anatomical names for various regions of the male genitalia.

This includes the perineum, which is apparently the "male clitoris", the interesting wrinkly bit of skin between the end of the balls and the beginning of the asshole. For women, this is mainly just a bony bit that bruises if you're too skinny, but not for men, it seems.

I once knew a girl who described a large bodybuilder as having a body that "felt like one giant, erect cock." So yes, I must say, a giant, erect cock feels rather like a miniature bodybuilder. The skin is soft, what's beneath is hard and pulsates with small movements like the smaller tendons and fibres in a very lean bodybuilder's arm.

Pierre took his time about putting his miniature bodybuilder to its appropriate use. The lingering moments he spent in fondling my breasts, running his tongue around my ass and flicking it across my clitoris, all reassured me more and more than I had picked the right man to be rapidly experiencing the First Time with.

I had to consciously refrain from reaching orgasm within five seconds of feeling his massive cock snugly slipping inside me. I will not attempt to describe how it feels, because English is woefully short of subtle language for sex. (Unlike, say, ancient Greek or Roman Latin, which got very specific about who was doing what to whom with what, and where.)

The earth didn't move. It didn't have to. I just had an explosive orgasm, with every muscle of my body. An explosive orgasm is as descriptive as it needs to get, really.

Pierre himself took his time about it. This is rare for a man, but the whole point of picking him over any number of other men was the high probability that he knew how to do it.

That was the end of my virginity. And it's funny, but when I think back on it, there are two moments in my life that have been such great triumphs they fill me with a lasting sense of purpose and *joie de vivre* that continue to echo throughout my life.

One was losing my virginity to a stranger named Pierre. And the other is none of your business.

For now.

"Do You Have A Toothbrush?"

Lee Lien Mingmei

The deliciousness of an unexpected sexual encounter takes a long time to fade from memory.

She used the unlikely name Bernadette as her western name, although her Chinese one was melodious and charming. The virgin saint's name actually fit her well, though she was in her late twenties. She wore her hair short and dressed in a demure yet silky fashion. She was serious about her personal development as an attendant in a home for mentally retarded children. The pay was dismal but she derived great personal fulfillment from it. She was good at it and the children responded to her evident passion for helping them. Her dream was to create her own facility some day.

She had a lithe figure with breasts that appeared larger than those usually found on Asian women. They later turned out to be supple, malleable and moved ever so rhythmically when caressed by hand and tongue.

We were acquaintances through the meetings of a few charitable functions where we were both donating some time and effort. Our first meeting was the most significant. As she came up and introduced herself and spoke with gentle passion about her commitment to the charity at hand, there was a powerful scent of spiritual and sexual harmony that comes when people have instant rapport. Her husband said hello and just ambled off. Our conversation was intense. As is common, we exchanged business cards. I left with a lingering yet tenuous yearning that we might meet again.

From time to time we met at public events, but nothing matched the first meeting. Our other encounters consisted only of innocuous conversation.

Her call early one evening took me completely by surprise. She and her husband were living at home with her parents, two sharing a room meant for one; they were struggling with finances since her job paid so little. Something had caused an uproar in the family and she wanted to come over and use my couch for two nights, if it was alright with me. It was, though I had no tingle or rush; I just assumed it was as she stated and it wouldn't interfere with my independent life. What was a few days? I had an extra couch and didn't need to give up my bedroom.

At about 9.30 pm she arrived. She brought a few things and hoped she wouldn't be a bother. I set up the couch as a bed with a sheet, a big puffy comforter and a few pillows, then gave her the TV remote and showed her where her bathroom was. She gladly accepted a pair of my blue cotton pyjamas, button top and pants with elastic waist, and said they would be fine. When I had to show her how to adjust the aircon as she climbed into the soft "bed", I saw they actually fit nicely.

By 11 pm, I was asleep in bed with my door closed. At 2 am, something stirred. She quietly came in and gently woke me, "Do you have a toothbrush?"

"At 2 am you want to brush your teeth? Why at this hour?"

"I want to thank you and give you a blow job."

I wasn't sure what I had heard. Reflexively and almost inaudibly, I said "Okay." I got up and found her a new toothbrush and went back to bed. Now what? There was no anticipation or sense of expectation. Maybe because it was late, and dark. The only light came from under the door of the bathroom and that soon clicked off.

I turned over on my back as she got on the foot of the bed. She faced me, gently resting on the backs of her bent legs. Her pyjama top was now open and as she reached down, I sat up. In one spontaneous moment she fell easily backward and in almost one motion, her pyjama pants slid off. We came into each other body to body, mouth to mouth, completely interlocked.

It was volcanic and overwhelmingly intimate. Our pulsating motion was so intense that we both reached climax in minutes, but just before I ejaculated I slid out and cupped my hand between her legs, spurting out warm seed which mingled with the flow of her wetness. We were in convulsions of rapture. I moved my warm hand up her thighs, along her belly, gently rolling up her receding breasts as I pushed up, let go, and held her now smeared wet face in an embrace. We could hardly breathe. Ever so slowly I rolled over and she slid on top of me, both dripping in our own sweat and juices. We stayed that way for hours. Glued by our passion. Though the air conditioning purred, its chill made no difference to our entangled rapture.

Club Koyaanisqatsi

Miss Izzy

"On a diet?" she asked, giving him a lopsided smile that spoke of contempt and a gross fascination with his bulbous shape.

She was beyond beautiful, with straight, smooth dark hair tied tightly into a French braid and a body of toned, tensed muscles wrapped over a slender frame. Her pale breasts nearly spilled out of an indecently buttoned blouse.

He had been inspecting the chocolate bars on the whole-foods shelf: 100% organic, high in protein, antioxidants, good cholesterol—but laden with three hundred calories, the equivalent of one meal under his new diet. He looked at her glumly, a little confused. She raised an eyebrow; "Well?" it said. Her smile taunted him for an answer.

"Uh ... yes. On a diet."

She chuckled audibly before stopping herself by jamming her teeth on the end of her thumbnail. "Sorry, sorry. I couldn't help it. But I know exactly what your problem is," she told him.

Kenneth didn't know whether to feel angry and insulted or flattered that a woman like her was even interested enough in him to say more than, "Hi!" Yet, an undeniable interest in her eyes suggested something beyond a cruel desire to make fun of him. Perhaps his embarrassment at being seen like an alien object showed on his face because her expression softened. She apologised.

"I know how you feel," she said. "And I know what you need to do. You need to stop being afraid of life. When the excitement of other things becomes the chief motivation in your life, then the lazy comfort of food is less of a necessity."

Kenneth looked at her blankly for a moment before he managed to absorb what she had just said. "Uh ... okay," he replied lamely.

"Come to my place for dinner tonight. Forget your diet. I'll make sure of it," she said smiling, her lips curling with excitement. Kenneth swore that look she gave him was carnivorous, but he pushed it out of his mind almost immediately. She pulled out her loyalty card for a club called Koyaanisquatsi, with her name and number on it, and told him to call her later in the evening.

"Just before nine. Let me get my apartment in order and cook up a little something before you arrive. Don't play me out," she said, turning on her heel and walking away.

He had turned up that night, and the last couple of weeks had seen the most bizarre days of his otherwise mundane existence. Club Koyaanisquatsi had turned out to be an exclusive place for sexual perversions of all manner, and although it had frightened him initially, making him run away, he came back soon enough.

The decision had been sealed when, the morning after his

daunting first introduction to the club, his chaste girlfriend Lynette called before dawn to tell him how much she loved him and to ask if he would please quickly decide on a date for their marriage so she could have her fucking babies and they could use her dying mother's money to live together in a flat somewhere in the arse of Singapore.

Club Koyaanisquatsi frightened his balls off, but it was a fantasy like he'd never experienced before. He put down the phone on Lynette with a smouldering anger inside, not against the poor girl, but against himself. That he had been so afraid all his life and stayed fearful of "attempting the uncharted experiences of physical sensation." That was the exact phrase Vanessa used, and he quite liked the sound of it.

It was a Thursday night, and Kenneth was having problems finding something he was comfortable playing with to add another stamp to his loyalty card. He'd exhausted the number of times he could claim credit for getting his bottom paddled by the newly initiated dominatrix, and he'd done with the horsehair whip as well. That, he thought was quite unpleasant and unexciting but no worse than getting a tattoo.

He looked at the girls lying on the dining tables, having sushi eaten off their bodies, and wished he could just do that. It actually looked exciting and relatively easy, though he wasn't quite sure about the wasabi on the balls. But people had to invite you to serve them and only the most gorgeous ever had any opportunity at all.

Vanessa came into the room and spotted him almost

immediately; she had a knack of doing that. Kenneth felt like her pet project of late. It seemed that she was adamant about turning him into one of the Koyaanisquatsi clergy: the sexiest, most louche individuals in the "family"—a term Vanessa liked to use when referring to the members of the club. He thought she was out of her mind, of course. Those people were like her: rich, sexy, and when they weren't spanking each other in lion cages, they lounged over expensive cigars late into the night and discussed Derrida and the possibility of comprehending the breadth and depth of infinity.

She invited him to have dinner with her, and as they passed the statue of a gargoyle that he thought looked vaguely like an armadillo, he dropped some money into it, making sure to do so only when Vanessa was clearly not looking. He was ashamed of the paltry amount of money he could afford to put into the donation box. No matter how often Vanessa told him the club was rich enough, that money was not an issue, he would always feel ashamed of being unable to contribute more.

They settled at a table, and as soon as they took their seats, a girl in a kimono came over and threw herself onto the table. As her body hit the black marble, her arms and legs splayed and her kimono burst open to offer her naked body. Another girl followed and started laying sushi on her. Kenneth had gone through the whole routine every night he'd come to the club, but he still cringed when the wasabi was slathered onto the girl's clit.

As soon as the girl had thrown herself onto the table and assumed a comatose demeanour, a few other people joined them at the long bench, seating themselves politely on either side of the girl, everyone sitting cross-legged on tatami mats. Vanessa broke the silent anticipation by saying grace: "Thank you for the body upon which we nourish ourselves, for her absolute worthiness as an individual, and ours, and our right to help ourselves to all the pleasures of life. The right to get drunk on the beauty of our existence and celebrate its autonomy from death and eternity. Amen."

She picked up a piece of glistening raw tuna on rice, dipped it into the puddle of soy sauce poured into the cavity of the girl's belly, and pressed it against the pearl of wasabi on her clit. Everyone else followed suit, eating neatly and slowly, occasionally pausing to sip from little cups of sake. Some people engaged in polite conversation about nothing much; the couple across from Kenneth seemed to be contemplating inviting the bagel-delivery boy from their office to the club. Then the lady beside Vanessa decided to break the prevailing protocol and started eating sushi off the girl's body without her chopsticks. She climbed on top of the girl and picked a piece off her shoulder with her teeth, dipped it in soy, rubbed it against her clit and tilted her head, allowing it to slide easily into her mouth. Everyone followed suit. Everyone except Kenneth: he never felt worthy, no matter how many times Vanessa intoned that prayer of hers.

There were seven people participating now, all licking, sucking, fondling, jostling one another, kissing one another. But mostly they teased the girl, and she tried her best to bear the sensations without revealing that she felt anything. Some of the men had taken their cocks out and were slapping them on

151

her face, her breasts. The woman who had been sitting beside Vanessa now sat on the girl's face, and Kenneth felt embarrassed for the man trying to get his cock into the girl. At the same time, Kenneth wished he could be the one pushing his cock into her tight wet pussy.

The girl on the table was so petite and so pretty, she looked barely eighteen. He wondered who she was and how she'd ended up here. But she was no slave. He saw her lips curl into a self-satisfied smile as the man above her gasped, his cock having finally managed to force itself into her.

Vanessa asked to look at Kenneth's card, and he slipped it to her uncertainly. She had a habit of suggesting, quite forcefully, he try things he wasn't ready for. But then again, if she never had, he would never have done anything. He had been to clubs like Koyaanisquatsi before, and all ever he'd done previously was sit in a corner nursing his drink with a confused erection in his pants.

Vanessa looked at him with a glimmer in her eye when she saw he'd used up all the Level One tasks, then nodded knowingly to herself. She pointed to the medical table, and Kenneth looked at her, his eyes wide with fear, mouth partially open in silent protest, head shaking in small, terrified turns.

"Trust me," she said. "You won't get hurt. Have you gotten hurt yet?"

Kenneth thought angrily to himself that he most certainly had, but then remembered that, to Vanessa, getting hurt meant being mutilated beyond hope of recovery without medical care. Anything that the body could get over naturally was acceptable.

"Look, it's the easiest thing for you to do at this point in time. All you have to do is take this," she said, handing him a little blue pill.

"But I don't have erectile dysfunction," he insisted, a little distraught at not knowing what manner of weirdness was about to happen to him.

"Surely, when something good is offered, you don't reject it. You might think it's nonsense now, but you'll see it isn't. Why do we have to keep on having this conversation every time something new is introduced to you?" she asked, her voice both pleading and tired. She pushed a lock of hair from her face in frustration and half-glared at him, her eyes saying, "Why are you being so difficult? It's your freedom I'm fighting for here."

Kenneth looked at her, feeling a little ashamed. He knew she wasn't completely right about certain things, but he was certain of having become less and less afraid of life with every session. The problem of his impending marriage to Lynette was also becoming clearer to him. He didn't need her any more, not her constant worry about having children or her indelible hold on his financial security. Alright, she had money, not that much, and he didn't. Fuck it. He shot down half a Spiegelau glass of whisky on the rocks, took the pill and went to the table.

Vanessa watched as a young boy and girl came to remove his clothing. She could see how insecure he still was about his body, and rightly so, she thought. The girl pulled his pants down unfeelingly and Vanessa felt pity at how soft he was around the stomach, how the hair grew in patches just above his crotch.

He had an awful slouch and slightly sallow skin on the areas he never allowed to see the sun.

Worse, Vanessa thought, he was the only one in this whole damn place that looked truly naked, in the saddest sense of the word, when he had his clothes off. He wanted to be like the other men and women, to be like her. Wrap himself up in a Calvin Klein body, burnish that body with some artificial bronzing, be moulded like a Tinseltown star in the gym. He needed a good diet and a workout every so often, but there was something raw in his soft, unpolished body that drew Vanessa to him. His body both fascinated and repulsed her.

She told him to lie on the table, and uncertainly, but with utmost resignation, he did. He lay there and said nothing, even though he felt slightly ridiculous, the sensation of ridicule increasing as Vanessa strapped him onto the table with thick leather belts, securing his calves and his shoulders to the cold metal slab. By now, the pill's contents were starting to course through his blood, and he had an erection as massive as any he had ever had in his life and felt certain he was going to have a heart attack.

He expected Vanessa to leave him in a moment, like she always did after she'd made sure he wasn't going anywhere, and for another girl to take over. But this time, she leaned over him, her face so close he could feel her breath on his cheek. She smiled and asked, "So, are you any different now?"

"I don't get what you mean."

"Now. From then. Two weeks ago."

"I don't know," he replied. "I mean, I don't know what

you mean."

"Liar," she said, her voice laden with malice as she climbed over him and hitched up the bottom third of her dress. "You do not debase my efforts *just like that* by being an idiot. Think. It's been different, hasn't it? You'd have come in your pants two weeks ago if I did this to you," she said, lowering herself over him. Her perfume was strong and it made him dizzy, and as unlikely as it was, he got even harder.

She pulled out a slender knife hidden in her garter and pressed the blunt edge against his chest. She smiled when he cringed and looked up at her, afraid. She lowered herself onto him, her labia against his erection, and he felt just what she was like for the first time. His hardness pressed against her but wouldn't go in, he was slightly too big. He felt embarrassed. He knew he would come soon, too soon for Vanessa's liking, and he would feel so ashamed. It was absurd, everything was. He wasn't like one of *them;* all these people had monstrous egos, and rightly so. He was a little turd their priestess had taken a fancy to, and that was all he would ever be in this place.

But being Lynette's little turd would be worse, he reminded himself, and closed his eyes, trying to think about other things so he wouldn't come.

He felt her press herself against him, trying to push his erection in and in, but she remained closed. She pushed harder, he felt uncomfortable, she was too dry. But she didn't care, forcing herself hard onto him. She was wet inside, and he went in easily the moment she'd forced herself open. Her crotch slammed painfully against his, and she gasped with satisfaction. Looking at her under half-closed lids, he saw her pull the knife away from his chest and place it slowly, sharp edge down, against the area just above his collar bone.

"Don't move," she said. "It will hurt."

The middle of the table split open vertically, just the bottom half where his legs were, just enough to pull his buttocks apart. Vanessa remained straddled over him, her knife against his flesh, rocking herself on his erection. His heart was pounding, and he felt the adrenaline rush soaking his system and chilling his body. He both loved and hated the fear of waiting for the unknown to happen: he had gotten used to the whipping and the spanking, but this he couldn't anticipate. He'd never been on one of the tables before.

He couldn't think about that though; under the table, something or someone was running a piece of wet, cold cloth between his buttocks, and he couldn't stop himself from shivering with anxiousness and embarrassment. No one had wiped his buttocks since he was three, and it made him feel humiliated. It went the entire length, from the base of his spine to the base of his balls: up and down, again and again. Wet, cold, and slow.

He lay as still as he could, trying his best not to cringe, although he badly wanted to make the face he was in the habit of making when he'd down gulps of very strong, very bad rum. Then the wiping stopped, and he could feel the end of a cold, metal dildo tease the entrance to his bum. The dildo slipped in a little, pulled out, then slipped in a little again. And it continued like that for some time, until he was tormented with fear and anticipation. He wanted it inside, but he knew it was going to hurt, and he still didn't like pain very much. It wasn't in his personality; he had the singular inability to endure pain passively, as Vanessa and the rest were capable of doing.

He bit his lip and repeated in his head that everything would be fine. That was one of the ironclad rules of the club: no one died, no one got irreversibly hurt unless they did it to themselves. Yes, everything would be fine.

Then it happened: the dildo forced itself completely into him, and he felt it tearing his flesh, just so slightly, but the small wound seared through his body, and he bit his lower lip until it bled to distract him from the pain. It was a pity he couldn't have an orgasm there and then, he thought, because he'd read somewhere orgasms were great for numbing pain while they lasted.

But he didn't come, and he would have to wait some time to find out. At that moment, he was only thankful for the straps holding him down. He would have gasped and jerked himself into the knife otherwise. The sharp pain seared through his anal orifice and he could feel himself starting to cry. This was truly horrid. He knew what had gone inside him, he'd seen it before. It looked completely innocent when you observed it—the smoothest, wettest dildo ever—but it hurt, bloody hell. It hurt.

Vanessa looked at him, slightly concerned for perhaps the first time, but erased any trace of this emotion almost instantaneously. She'd clearly lost her desire to carry on and unsaddled him, putting the knife back into the holster on her garter and smoothing her skirt down. She looked at him for a moment before she decided to remove the dildo from his bottom.

"You didn't say stop," she said, looking at him curiously, pleased and a little triumphant.

"No. I suppose I didn't. I've become so used to believing everything will be fine," Kenneth panted when he had recovered and Vanessa had removed the straps binding him. She nodded her head like she had heard that said many times before, then walked away distractedly without even bidding him good night.

He put on his clothes in a daze and decided to go home. He would normally have lingered for a while after he had fulfilled his criteria for the night, watching things other members did to themselves and wondering how they managed it. He'd look at them attempting stunts he'd never imagined: real whips, real knives, iron rods smouldering from a fresh fire. Suddenly, he wanted to try them all, each and every one. More and more, the appeal of Club Koyaanisquatsi grew on him, and the fear those practices held for him waned. What had been foreign and dangerous, machines and mindsets that threatened to topple the order of what he believed to be right, felt freeing and energising.

This world of the club, he decided, was no worse and no better than the one he was casting off. He wasn't so afraid any longer of things that couldn't actually hurt him, or even of things that could.

Self-Portrait
With Three Monkeys

Chris Mooney-Singh

He kept thrashing and crashing around on top of her, making the required efforts to reach his record-time orgasm. If there had been an Olympic category for 'wham-bam-thank-you-Ma'am' sex, he would have easily made the team, she thought. It happened all too often: the big build-up over dinner and hanging out at Bar None had led to another unsatisfying conclusion. Now the performance was over. He withdrew himself, limp and spent, rolled off to his side of the bed, sweating on the sheet. Francisca had learned not to expect fireworks, yet she did hope for slow, practiced arousal—or perhaps a little humour along the way.

He let out a deep yawn. "Very tired, lah."

He looked across the room, taking in the easel next to the dresser. "Hey, you also paint, ah. Very sexy! This one, who, ah?

She cringed. *Oh God! What to tell him?* But before Francisca could answer, he had turned over and was off to count sheep or naked pole-dancers, or whatever he did to fall asleep. She half-muttered to herself, "*Yes, why don't you make yourself at home, 'Stud'!*"

He was asleep now, but his words echoed on like the ghost of an insincere idea. Did he not see her resemblance in the unfinished portrait? *Well, what do you expect! You didn't hook up with an art lover, did you?* Francisca's sagging, forty-eight-year-old body had been raging and partying for years, progressing like flaming octane through the clubber's long, dark night of the soul.

She left the bed and went to clean up in the bathroom. When she returned, she sat down at the dresser-mirror. Soon, the numbskull sparrows would be up in the Flame of the Forest tree outside her window. Before long, the tropical sun would be getting her and the workers off to their office blocks for another day's spreadsheets and marketing campaigns and the food courts would be queued up with hung-over monsters craving for *kopi* and *kaya* toast. Her mouth tasted of cigarettes and sour margaritas.

She looked at the black waterfall of her hair draped over the red silk gown embroidered with tigers. Ah, her smeared mascara. At the end of her life, would she be still picking up guys in bars until the last round of drinks? She really was too old for this now. Her biological time-bomb was beginning to tick louder between heartbeats. Too old for kids. She had some cash in the bank for a trip or two, but to where and with whom? The "who" in bed, reflected in the mirror, was just another jerk in post-coital whale-slumber. The sex and booze had done the job for him: out like a light. *Typical!* But she was still turned on like flashing neon.

Next to her on the easel was the nearly finished canvas. She stood up to look at it—a voluptuous nude. She flashed back to the mirror—then to the canvas, then the mirror again. She undid the red silk dressing gown at the waist and opened herself for objective appraisal. *Who is this person? Do I still know her?* The breasts were certainly not as perky as a twenty-year-old's and she saw the evidence of a little—dare she say it—paunch! *My God! A man's word for a woman's tummy. What is happening to me?* There was some shadow of fuzz on the upper lip, a stray hair or two on the chin these days growing faster between tweezer attacks. Yes, Francisca was losing her soft feminine edge to a menopausal creature known as Fran the frump. She was becoming thick brush strokes, like a Rouault painting: man-solid, deep-vowelled.

Yet it wasn't the bagginess of her skin that disturbed her so much as what it all stood for: no partner, no family, no orthodox identity except an executive position which was now under attack from those "Hello Kitties" scratching at her heels. She had to keep on top, swat them like flies … She was known as a tough nut to crack in her industry, but under that hard shell, she was sensitive: someone who tried to manifest her realness through one-woman shows in a friend's art gallery. Alas, she was only a part-time artist in a Sunday-painter country with little art appreciation or market potential. Francisca reached for the cleanser and tissues and began clearing up the mascara-disaster area.

"Oh God," she shuddered, closing her eyes in fright. She stood up, turning to look at the bed where the whale-man was snoring. She turned her back, leaning against the window, looking at the self-portrait. She needed comforting, so she closed her eyes again and let a well-trained finger stray below the embarrassing belly to the bearded-lady lips of herself and, imagining her finger as a delicate paintbrush, started doing what she normally did at the easel: shutting out the left-over white noise of her workday to look for that other Face, the ideal woman within herself. She then began to re-create its lines and contours, working her finger-brush this way and that.

The sexual heat began to build like the first kindling placed on a match-blaze. It grew gradually with focus and effort to twig-bright redness. She kept her eyes closed and felt her left calf muscle going taut as a bowstring as her body remembered this fiery dance for one—all the while dwelling on the image of the younger woman she knew so well, the one she had starved, exercised, then bounced through nightclubs and parties with European men and big expense accounts.

This laughing, joking woman had been the wild one with a reputation for doing the most daring things in beachfront chalets all weekend long. She warmed to that bright young image as she worked the finger-brush, painting a face like a miniature portrait on the red ruby of her clitoris—a face all lips and tongue now finding the sweet-spot. Rising on her toes she embraced the full force of her orgasm, shuddering with hot, delicious stabs.

Feeling revitalized, she imagined a new beginning with a clean slate and felt her feet soften into the floor again. As she opened her eyes to the reddened cheeks of a woman flashed sideways in the mirror, Francisca realized she was still that empowered woman. She was not down-and-out. She didn't need the man-whale beached in the bed behind her. No one had ensnared her in any domestic tussle. She had a job, she had her house (almost paid off), she had her CPF savings. All was not lost. Above all, there was her art. Yes, that had always served even if it didn't make any money. She could still paint, could still create. Francisca still had a way of being honest with herself, despite the prowling diversions of her tiger-woman lifestyle.

The morning light was just beginning to do its little halo-dance around the outlines of apartment blocks. A shaft of it began to walk a finger through the slit in the curtain. Francisca took it as a signal to action and stepped up to the canvas. She lifted a brush from the Chinese inkstand on the table next to the easel where she kept her materials. She looked at the green soapstone piece carved with three monkeys ascending a mountain. The pool at the bottom was the muddy pot that she now dabbed into like a water-bird taking a morning drink.

How strange! The climbing monkeys now seemed to be laughing and joking. *How foolish one can be, possessed by moods and darkness.* Francisca grabbed her palate and felt like flinging it up like pizza dough, but restrained herself. Instead, she squeezed out some colour onto its paint-scarred face, then began intoning her mock mantra as she did before commencing any work at the easel: *See no evil, hear no evil, speak no evil.*

Such a silly saying, yet for her it meant that she could turn a blind eye to the necessary sins of her day job. She didn't have

163

to listen to the bleating voices of family expectations and she wouldn't ever have to speak again to this latest jerk slumbering in her bed, once she sent him off without breakfast. She focused her eyebrows as if she was a mathematician searching for a way to crack the formula.

With her brush, she added a few final touches around the lips and softened the lines of the painted tummy, then signed the portrait in the bottom right hand corner. Then she moistened her finger with her own wetness, dipped it in the red paint on the palate and, with a flourish, dotted the "i".

Walking The Dog

Gerrie Lim

"The first time I did it, I cried," explains Emily. "For everybody, there is always a first time, where you get upset. Where you feel like you're dirty, you're selling your body." She flicks stray bangs off her forehead, revealing a furrowed brow, and lodges a fresh smoke between her pursed lips. She's twenty-eight years old, a Chinese Singaporean who grew up in the old pre-war shophouse district around Lavender Street.

"In the early days, I had problems talking with the customers. The first time I dressed up, I was terrible. I dressed like an ah lian, a village girl. And I talked very loudly. Sapphire, my agency owner, guided me a lot. My hair was terrible, all bunched up and curly like Maggi Mee instant noodles, and Sapphire told me it was ugly and made me straighten it. She told me not to talk as if I was going to have a fight, or to wear platforms or tight pants. She made me look through magazines. She taught me how to talk politely to the customers."

Sapphire laughs when reminded of this. "When Emily went out on her early assignments, her service was always bad. It was like hit-and-run, and the customers complained. I told her, 'How can you go to a customer and speak like a gangster?' She was so rude. I told her, 'The next time a customer complains, I won't use you anymore.' She's improved a lot since then."

Well, she must have, since she now commands S$700 to S$1,000 an hour, in part because she does the jobs the other girls won't do. Group sex, bondage and domination, whipping and spanking, hot wax and other forms of unusual punishment. There's a slight twist to her lips, a subtle pout that hints of cruelty, which lends a menacing aura to her not unattractive visage, one blessed with all the known attributes of classical Chinese beauty. Emily has an oval face with eyes and nose perfectly proportioned, set off with the kind of long black hair and pale, porcelain skin so very prized by Western men. A lot of her customers come from cities like London and Boston, places she has never been to and could barely find on a map ten years ago, when she began escorting at the age of nineteen.

"On my first job I was very frightened and didn't know what to do. I had to go straight to a hotel and I didn't know who would be answering the door. I didn't know how to do a massage or how to talk to a strange guy. The agency I was working for then didn't train me or anything. On that first job, when I knocked on the hotel room door, I actually covered the peephole so the man wouldn't see me!

"But the evening went smoothly. He was a foreign guy, an ang moh, a white man. Looked a bit like Brad Pitt. I didn't even have sex with him. He wanted to but I told him I was too nervous! He was nice about it. I finished the three hours of escorting and left. We just went out to dinner and talked. I remember that I didn't eat anything. I was terrified that he might drug my drink or my food. You never know what might happen when you're out with a total stranger. I even went on a job after that where they sent me to Brunei. But I made a U-turn and came back. I had never been on a plane before, I was so scared and I cried and cried.

"They were very nice about it. They paid me S$1,000 and sent me back. One thousand dollars, just to make a U-turn! But soon I started being able to have sex, with no problems. Nothing kinky, just straight sex. Now I've matured to the point where I will do anything."

Now, Emily works as a masseuse in a women's slimming salon during the day, and escorting is merely her night job. "I do body massage for ladies. I do facials too. I put mudpacks on their faces, scrub them, put them in machines that break down cellulite, and wrap them up like mummies. I went to beautician school too. Then, a customer gave me $5,000 to attend a make-up course. I went because he paid for it. But I realized I was more interested in beauty than in make-up."

So what's a beautician like her doing in a place like this? It's a rhetorical question made poignant by the fact that the area she grew up in happens to lie amid the very districts where the world's oldest profession first took root in Singapore. Large-scale commercial movements of women for the purpose of pleasure took place in the late 19th century, whereby Chinese girls were sent to Singapore, Malaysia, and Thailand to satisfy the growing numbers of male migrant laborers eking out a living in the ports. The historian James Francis Warren, in his book Ah Ku and Karayuki-San: Prostitution in Singapore, 1870-1940, notes that "the economic development of Singapore favored prostitution as the male population of the city greatly outnumbered the females: the gap was 1 female to 14 males in 1860 and this gender imbalance was to continue for the next seventy years."

Sex for sale is, of course, best known in Thailand, but Emily's place in the pecking order is at the opposite end of the spectrum from the hapless Burmese girls who still work the cheapest Bangkok brothels. No, Emily spends her evenings ensconced in five-star hotels, sipping Champagne and surveying the scenery from penthouse suites. There might well be a Japanese executive at hand who has paid handsomely for her services. And not necessarily for sex.

"One Japanese guy wanted me to treat him like a dog," Emily recalls. "He wanted me to see what was in the fridge and feed it to him. I would drip chocolate onto a saucer and make him eat it. Squash his head with my leg and make him eat a biscuit off the floor. Whip him. Walk him up and down on a leash. I brought my own dog leash, tied it around his neck, and made him walk around the whole hotel room. Then he had to pee like a dog, on the carpet. No sex. He masturbated himself.

"This was at seven o'clock in the morning! I got the call from the agency at 6.30 am It took one hour, and I was done by eight o'clock." She takes another drag of her cigarette.

Escorting is an outcall business, so Emily has to go out to work, unlike call girls who'll receive calls and then customers at their residences, like those fabulous New York call girls who work out of their Upper East Side apartments. "I meet clients at their hotel, talk to them and ask them whether they're comfortable with me and do they want to confirm the job," she explains cheerfully. "If they do, I will call back to the agency and let them know that I have arrived safely and have collected the booking." Different agencies charge different booking fees—it can be S$200 for a two-hour minimum, sometimes a four-hour minimum, or S$100 an hour for a three-hour minimum. This fee is collected by the girl and returned to the agency, in exchange for which she may get a cut, depending on the agency's policy.

The real money, however, lies in what transpires beyond that minimum period, where the girls will provide what in the parlance of the Singapore escort trade is discreetly termed "extra services." Usually in the S$300 to S$500 range, the fee is privately negotiated between the gentleman and his companion. None of it goes back to the agency—the girl keeps it as her tip.

"We are facilitating companionship, not marketing sex," is how one agency owner puts it. "What happens after the two or three or four hours of actual escorting are over, it's not for me to know. I don't know and I don't want to know." However, the agency makes money off this too, because the client has to "extend the booking" and he will then have to pay an extra S$100 or S$200 per the same hourly period. It is the girl's responsibility to collect this on behalf of the agency; the only money she's supposed to keep outright is her tip.

And the things they have to do, for that tip. Some escorting jobs don't involve sex at all. One lucky girl received a call at 7 am to meet with a gentleman for breakfast. All she did was have breakfast with him, and at the end of the meal he tipped her S$500. Emily remembers going out on a lot of non-sex jobs where she collected several hundred dollars each time. "I show them around. They will ask me for Singaporean food and we'll go to Newton Circus or things like that. If they want seafood, I'll bring them to the East Coast, which is nice because we can stroll along the beach after dinner. If they want some nightlife, I'll take them to Brix, at the Hyatt.

"Sometimes, if the customer books me for several hours, like six hours, I'll take them to Victoria Street, to show them the open concept food courts and to teach them how to order. We don't always do the air-conditioned places. It all depends on what my customers like, rather than what I want."

Sometimes, the dates have unexpected outcomes, somewhat hilarious and at her expense. "One guy booked me to accompany him to a Malay wedding. He asked me to dress nicely. I presumed he would take a taxi because I was thinking it was a wedding lunch or reception or something. So I dressed in black and wore a jacket. It was so warm. But he made me walk from the escort agency office to Orchard MRT station, and take the train to Bedok and then take a feeder bus! Can you imagine? So many people were looking at me and I felt so stupid, wearing a jacket and taking a bus and then sitting at the HDB void deck [the open-sided ground floor of a housing project, built by the Singapore government's Housing Development Board]. There I was, having my lunch and pretending to be his girlfriend. He was a local Malay guy. A Malay wedding in an HDB void deck!"

"I meet all the weird customers," Emily sighs. "One time, this guy booked me for escorting and we met at Furama Hotel, where he paid me the money and said, 'Okay, let's go.' I didn't know where he was taking me but I had already confirmed the job so I said okay. He took me to the Subordinate Courts! He said I had to pretend to be his girlfriend. His ex-girlfriend was there and he wanted me to be there just to provoke her. I was supposed to be his new girlfriend. I didn't have to say anything. I just sat through the entire hearing. I was terrified and embarrassed. I had never been to the courts before and here I was doing escorting in a courtroom! He tipped me S$200."

Even when there is no sex involved, Emily sometimes gets to role-play with clients who obviously have a rich fantasy life. Her favorite client, she says is an elderly gentleman. "Uncle Freddie. He's seventy or eighty years old. He would ask me to marry him and I would ask him for his bank account: 'Show me you can afford me first!' He would ask me to dance for him, seduce him. He would dance the Macarena! His dancing was stiff, like he was driving a car. But he always asks for me. No sex. I would give him a shower. He likes showers. And then I would talk to him. Tease and provoke him, 'Your dick is so big! Your dick grows so long!' He told me he takes Vitamin C with zinc and it makes his dick grow. It's fun! He would always book me on Saturdays and all I had to do was dance and keep him company. I like the fact that every Saturday is different, every Saturday would be a whole different story. It's quite fun, quite entertaining. And I don't have to have sex!"

But inevitably, Emily is frequently called for sex jobs, perhaps because she is highly adept at playing the requisite part. She thinks of herself as being paid to be an actress.

Fantasy sessions that accompany escorting are an elevated

kind of play-acting. Granted, there's a pathos to it. It's Emily's only chance to be a star. "I seem to get all the funny calls, like having to pretend to be a doctor or a dentist. They would give me a gown and I would have to inspect them. One client had me check and then polish his genitals with Colgate. I had to polish his balls with an electric toothbrush and then put Colgate on his dick. He told me to make a humming sound while I was doing it, like a buzzing sound, which would excite him even more. He came! That was so funny. One guy even bought a doctor's outfit complete with stethoscope and asked me to put it on. That's extending the booking beyond the usual S$300 minimum, and then he would tip me S$600!"

Another time, Emily was asked to simulate necrophilia. "It was his fantasy to make love to a corpse—I was asked to play dead," she giggles. "This guy was a pathologist or a coroner, he worked in a mortuary, and he made me pretend to be dead. I was naked and lay there pretending to be dead while he checked my body parts. He was lifting my arms and snooping around between my legs. He got an erection and wanted to have sex with me. I was lying there, holding my breath and pretending to be dead, and then I got worried that he might not use a condom so I suddenly got up and gave him a condom and then lay down to pretend to be dead again!

"He cried out 'Hey, you can't get up, you're already dead!' I put the condom on my stomach for him to take, and lay down again. It was weird because I was not to move a muscle while he had sex with me. He liked it that way. Of course, I couldn't have an orgasm since I couldn't move! But he pays good money—he paid me S$1,000 for that! If I can get the big tips, I'll pretend to be anything. I've had customers who would pay me S$1,000 just to sleep next to them. You just sleep only, that's it. I can sleep anywhere, so it's not a problem. They will extend the booking just to watch me sleep! Probably when they're working they hardly have time to see their wives or girlfriends sleep."

Emily is under no illusions about escorting. She has a husband who is ill and unable to work, and they have bills to pay. "If you think about the money, you can do anything, I believe that," she says firmly. "I can fake an orgasm, no problem."

What really turns Emily on these days, though, are the jobs that don't involve penetrative sex, that allow her to play out her own domination fantasies. "They pay me to whip them!" she enthuses. "I remember the first time I was sent out for a domination job. This was three years into my escorting career. This guy wanted to do an hour of massage and then after that we 'would discuss.' So, I went to the guy's home, confirmed the job and then the guy said he didn't want to have sex. I asked him what he wanted. He said he wanted domination. That was my first time. I didn't know what to do. I was shocked! People pay money to be whipped? I whipped him with a hanger. I didn't have anything else to whack him with, so I spanked him with the hanger.

"He said he wanted an additional service, a 'golden shower.' And I did it. I squatted over him and peed on his face. That's how he liked it. I even did a 'brown shower' once. This was for a European guy, a long time ago, at a hotel on Orchard Road. It was so late at night and I couldn't shit. He asked me drink black coffee and that helped. It took me so long to do it, though. I was in a bathtub with one leg on each side and his body underneath. I drank the coffee and jumped around a bit. I did it and he ate it. I shat into his mouth. It felt disgusting. I just think of the money and don't think of what I'm doing."

But there's one thing Emily has not yet done—the so-called "tiger show," which is the local term for a live sex show. "I have no problem with the idea of doing that," she says, "but I don't want anyone to tape it and circulate it. There have been guys who have videotaped girls and the girls end up crying. You never know what they do with the film. They might put it on the Internet."

We all have our sexual boundaries, explains Emily. Even for someone like her, whose comfort zone extends beyond that of most people. Emily becomes quite animated when she talks about her kinkier clients. "This Burmese guy had me tie him up and fill up the bathtub and then put his head in like I was going to drown him," she recalls. "I also did one guy in Bukit Timah who was bit of a pervert. He wanted to be a slave. He had me dress up in high heels and a short skirt and he would kiss my toes and lick my toes and then lick my four-inch high heels and then he wanted to use my high heels to squish his balls. And then, flip him upside down so he could eat his own sperm."

She leans back, gesticulates with her arms. "I had to poke the stiletto heel on his ass. I had to hold him, sit on a high stool and support his back with one leg while using the other leg to poke his anus—with my stiletto heel. So I'm pushing his back up with my thighs and legs, and he's lying with his legs up, and he masturbates and comes—into his own mouth. I did all this while smoking a cigarette!"

And when they want to be seriously violated, she'll do that too. "One guy wanted me to roll him with a rolling pin and then play with an egg blender on his privates. Then, he got out a big vibrator. He was tied up and he liked to be tortured with it, especially around his genitals. I also used candle wax but I wouldn't know if he was in pain or not because I gagged his mouth. I tied him up, whipped him, used paper clips to clip his balls, his dick, his nipples, everywhere. I would go back and tell the agency boss, and we would have a good laugh. If I couldn't laugh about it, I think I would have gone mad by now.

"I have issues from my childhood. My brother and sister would hang me upside down and cane me. If I didn't do the housework properly or if I didn't finish a task, they would cane me. My house has these ceiling hooks for hanging baby cots, and they hung a chain down, tied my legs, hung me upside down and caned me. I hated it so much. Now I cane people to take revenge!"

The violence, however, cuts both ways. She learned, rather traumatically, that she is not naturally submissive.

"I can dominate but I cannot receive," she says. "There was one customer, Richard, he wanted to smack me on the backside. Just for five minutes, and he would give me S$500. But I couldn't take it. I was crying and crying. I got so upset not because of the pain but because of my childhood memories. That was the hardest job I've ever done.

"I have had customers who were somebody in their

companies, heads of departments, and they would always like to be a slave. They wanted to make me coffee, massage me, bathe me. They even wanted me to humiliate them in public, which is something that I don't mind doing. I would scold them in public, tell them they're useless, things like that. Tell them they are my slave and must carry my shopping bags, scold them stupid and slow. I don't think of anything but the money, so it's kind of fun.

"I've also done strangling. I let the guy's head rest between my legs then I cross my legs together and apply pressure. I'll go out there with my colleague, Jasmine. We take turns and make sure the guy's still in one piece. If you know the tactic—how to hold somebody like that while applying pressure—you won't kill him. I don't have any kind of training in martial arts. You just have to focus. As long as you don't snap the neck, you will never kill a person.

"These jobs," she shrugs, "are about re-enacting my childhood."

Expeditions In
The Twilight Zone

Emilio Malvar

Years ago, I occasionally made trekking expeditions to Sabah in East Malaysia, a more intriguing state than those on the peninsula itself. These expeditions involved a few days' walk in a wilderness, usually with a mountain to scramble up. At the end of such a trip, I found myself in Kota Kinabalu, staying in a more elaborate hotel than I normally bothered with. Down in the basement, near the car-park area in the nethermost region of this grand establishment, was what was euphemistically termed a "health centre".

I had not patronised such an establishment before and was not quite sure what to expect. The room was poorly lit, the effect intended obviously being a sombre tranquillity or, perhaps, seductive gloom. It contained a mattress and a washbasin and not much else. I undressed, except for my underpants, then lay down, as only seemed sensible. Eventually a smallish woman appeared; because of the dark, I couldn't make out anything about her looks other than her size. In due course, as I grew more accustomed to the dim lighting and as we grew acquainted with each other, I came to discover she was a Filipina, working overseas like so many others.

This masseuse was a woman of around thirty with longish hair. It was difficult to judge her features because of the sombre ambiance, but her manner appeared stern, perhaps the consequence of reserve or shyness. Nonetheless, she gave my near-naked body a good hard look, especially the middle zone, and indicated that I should remove my underpants, which she presumably found more offensive than my genitalia. She then abruptly offered me coffee or tea. Thereafter, reluctantly emitting a few gruff pleasantries, she began to massage me, working a little indifferently with oil over most of my torso and limbs. Conversation was limited, partly because of mutual miscommunication and partly because the manner of this particular Filipina (her name, she reluctantly conceded, was Concepcion) was initially very serious, as if she were a doctor confronted with a terminal case. She did not seem very sure of either me or herself. Her voice sounded low, almost gravelly. I could hardly see her, even when I looked back over my shoulders, lying as I was in the typical massage position, face down on the mattress.

Concepcion set to work in a perfunctory manner, as if she were none too keen to touch human flesh. She avoided my shoulders, which happened to be sore and blistering from sunburn; not, as she told me afterwards, out of consideration for any pain I might have felt, but because she thought they might be infected. We talked a little about her life and family. She was divorced; divorced, moreover, with two youngish children who required a maid to look after them while she was at work. "Hundreds and hundreds a month," she griped. Twisting my head over my shoulder, I could see her grimace. Concepcion leant forwards to judge my reaction to this disclosure. Now I could see that she bore a slight scar at the corner of her mouth, as if she had been slashed by a knife. Perhaps reflecting on the injustices of the world, she lapsed into silence. Uncertain as to how matters would develop, I myself slipped into a doze.

I woke to feel a finger tracing a circle or two round my anus. A small, oily hand then moved forward a little to brush my testicles. Meeting with no opposition from me, the small hand began to knead them and then, increasingly emboldened, pushed further still to work on my male member, squeezing it more and more confidently as it responded and I lifted my body a little to accommodate this pleasant procedure. Suddenly it was clear to me that a new chapter was about to open in my sexual life, which had never proceeded in a smooth, unfolding manner but in fits and starts, like events in the quantum world, lurching randomly into sudden life and equally sudden annihilation.

Concepcion now seemed more urgent and interested. She suggested, though still nervously, that I might like something in addition to her half-hearted massaging of my back and shoulders. I turned to face her and asked what she had in mind. She made her offer of an extra, her *special*. This was to mouth my penis which, although it had originally met with her diffidence, was nonetheless erect. "But you must wear a condom," she said, with the firmness of a primary-school teacher instructing a child. She then disappeared for what seemed a long time. Returning

179

suddenly, she pointed to my trinity. "You washed it just now?" she asked, pausing a moment. I nodded. Kneeling before me, she tried to unroll a condom onto the relevant part of my body, making a hash of the job. "Quick, you do it," she said, giving me a small push with one hand while offering the rubber with the other.

I obliged and she started to work with her tongue. Abruptly changing her approach, she told me to lie down on my back, straddling me on all fours and swivelling her body around so that I was staring at her rear. She peered at me between her legs. "You do to me."

"What?" I said.

"You ..." She contorted her upside-down face, searching for the right word. We looked at each other for a few seconds, mutually non-plussed. She waggled her bottom and stuck out her tongue, making circular movements with her head. "Ah", I said and focused on her backside, my nose level with her entry and exit points. Her anus, a few centimetres away, was pinkish-brown and puckered round the edge. It was neat and charming enough as far as anuses go, and apparently very clean, but I was not greatly attracted to the reciprocal tongue exercises she had proposed. "No," I said. Peeking through her legs, her face registered an upside-down version of disappointment. Anus-licking or something of that nature was apparently her particular domain, being relatively safe and uncomplicated.

I renegotiated for a more conventional mode of sexual expression, in which I could be more vigorously engaged.

The lady illustrated an extreme nervousness over actual

intercourse: not repulsion or inhibition at the deed itself, but fear that someone would walk into the room which, following the perverse rule in these places, could not be locked. She was equally anxious that the business arrangement be carried out. "I haven't done this before," she announced breathlessly, meaning that she had never participated in full commercial sex. This surprised and slightly disconcerted me, as neither had I.

We embraced awkwardly in a standing position, but not without my somehow standing on one of her small feet. "Ouch," said my partner, recoiling and then re-embracing. Almost immediately, she had a hasty afterthought and disappeared. She scurried across the room and put the cubicle's pouffe against the door, first stuffing a towel underneath the door so that it would jam if anyone attempted to open it from the outside. This was a cautionary practice which I subsequently found to be near universal. She had obviously consulted her peers on this, even if she were feeling her way in a new field.

All this stumbling and bumbling did nothing to help me sustain my erection ... My partner obliged by poking and pulling at my trinity until vigour was restored. She lay down on the mattress. "Quick," she said again, hastily raising her short skirt and removing her knickers. We clumsily engaged after some more fumbling with limbs, clothes and organs. "Wait a minute," she said suddenly, expelling me in a peremptory manner before wriggling away, "the sheet will be stained." And indeed, the sheet was rucked up between us, part of our coital tangle.

She repositioned herself on the edge of the mattress so that the crucial zone was off the sheet and my lower limbs on the carpet. We started again. Meanwhile, somebody was clunking something down the passageway and talking in a low voice; probably the cleaning lady dragging a vacuum cleaner. "Oh," she said, over my shoulder, "they're coming in!" and ejected me once more. "No, its alright," she said as the noise passed. "Quick, come back," and she reinserted me.

We resumed our love-making which, despite her injunctions, was relatively prolonged. I had caught some of her nervousness and could not concentrate on the act. Also, my knees were getting sore from the friction from the carpet. "Can't we use the mattress?" I asked. "Yes, but I am so worried," said my partner. She pushed me away yet again and spread a towel, turning over to do so, and we re-engaged in that position. More indeterminate noises could be heard from outside the cubicle. Immediately, she squirmed and tried to say something about the door, but I held her tight despite her wriggling and, after some more confused communication, at long last consummation—at any rate, my consummation—was achieved.

"Phew," Concepcion said, getting up immediately and looking relieved, as if she had delivered a speech at some important occasion, like a wedding or college speech day. She seemed quite glad that it was all over. She scuttled about, straightening the sheet and restoring her underwear and so forth. I laughed at her amateurishness. "If you find it all so terrifying, don't do it."

She smiled at me happily. She was obviously relieved that I was not cross, considering the inelegance of our congress. "You should give me more because it was the first time", she said, taking advantage of the good humour. "You should be my boyfriend", she went on, persisting gently and repeating herself, "I have two children. I have to employ a maid to look after them while I am working here".

Concepcion then sat down next to me and began an unflattering examination of my body. "What's that?" she said suspiciously, pointing to some blemish in my groin area. "And that," she continued, looking critically at the sore patches on the inside of my knees, still stinging from the carpet. "I didn't want to touch your back," she said candidly, "It doesn't look nice." Then, worried that she had offended me, she said, "Sorry, don't mean that. You're not cross?" She peered at me intently, her face pushed close to mine to judge my expression in the gloom of the cubicle, like a cat hoping to wake its owner and be fed.

"Be my boyfriend." She leant forward enticingly. "Be my boyfriend," she wheedled again, pressing her body against mine. I leant back, but Concepcion moved further forward until she lay on top of me, her face still close to mine. She came off as much more confident with her clothes on. I found her urging appealing and instinctively wanted to protect her from her past mistakes and present predicament, but afterwards, my natural impulse to incorporate her into my life wore off. Her insistence might have indicated some stronger need for money for drugs than for her children. This thought made me wary of entering into a relationship because I was new to the guild of massage women like her and could not easily judge how stable or controlled they were. In any event, she lived in Sabah and I in Singapore, and my romantic urge to be involved with her soon faded in the pragmatic light of day outside the centre.

And so I entered into the world of the massage women—a twilight, windowless world, not of the extremes of eroticism but of the fumbling accommodation of desire with commerce ... and sometime intimacy, however awkward and confused.

This world was not, of course, the centre of my existence, as I had loves, work and interests outside the twilight. But it was much of their world. My experience in it was maybe five, at most ten per-cent of my life, if such things may be quantified. But it was significantly more emotionally, for I liked the massage women very much and saw in them as pleasant a division of my fellow human beings as any. Since I inevitably preferred some of the massage women much more over others and spent my time mostly with this preferred subset, my overall impression of them is no doubt a little slanted and rose-tinted, just as their experience of men was skewed towards the sensual and the strayer ... with not a few of the inadequate. Still, I felt soft towards them all and forgiving of their frailties, more forgiving than I would have been of people in other occupations.

On my return to Singapore after my encounter with Concepcion, I set about visiting the local 'health centres' and massage parlours, the first time I had ever set out on a campaign of exploratory promiscuity. Initially, I was a little wary of these twilight women, expecting drug-dependency, perhaps a parasitic or clinging tendency, or—worse—hell-cat behaviour and thievery. However, the first local centre that I visited was very reassuring. Situated in the middle of a big hotel, it was much better appointed than the car-park den in Kota Kinabalu (as behoved this clean and clinical Republic). It had its own shower with an expensively tiled floor and was pleasantly decorated, looking organized and neat with stacked towels, a high massage bed and almost no cigarette holes in the carpet. All this bespoke an almost domestic respectability, an efficient, business-like atmosphere with a faintly medical flavour because of the stacked towels and the general emphasis on hygiene.

While I was in the shower, a female entered the room and offered me a drink. I could not see her because of the frosting on the shower-cubicle door. She disappeared again while I lay down on the massage mattress. My masseuse appeared and started talking at once, firing off questions and setting to work on my back. She announced herself as Honey or Pussy or some such absurd professional name, but eventually, after a little pressing, admitted to being Caroline.

She was, as far as I could tell peering back over my shoulder, an ethnic Chinese woman in her thirties. I did not want to swivel round to stare at her rudely, as if assessing the quality of the goods I might consume. Caroline herself was quite formal in her interrogation, asking me at the beginning how she should address me and taking it on from there. Thus, we were both careful to preserve the ordinary decencies of social intercourse.

In time, I got to know Caroline a little, although my acquaintance with her was not as deep as with subsequent lovers in this particular twilight zone. She possessed a nondescript face but a pleasing figure and radiated sexual energy.

Caroline, as loquacious as Concepcion had been reserved and as experienced as the latter had been relatively innocent, gave me a rapid, light massage over my back and legs, accompanied by a lot of slapping as well as continuous chatter of interrogation. After less than ten minutes of this process, she ran her fingers and thumbs like a pair of five-legged spiders over my rear and inner thighs, circling my anus and tickling my testicles before kneading them slightly while groping for my penis.

"Do you want to turn over?" said the spider-lady. "That's a very quick massage," I said, though I was not complaining at the way proceedings were developing, just commenting on her directness. "Oh no," said Caroline, "there's more to come."

"Your approach is different," I noted.

"Oh no," she persisted, "I do not have an approach, I just do whatever is necessary. What do you want me to do?" Since she already had a proprietary grasp on my erect member, this was a polite but rhetorical question. So I asked her for full sex without a condom. She looked at me surprised. This was a test that I applied to the twilight women in my early days to see how sensible they were. Later, I dropped this insult to their intelligence and sense of responsibility.

"Oh no," said Caroline, not haggling and thus passing the test with flying colours, "you must wear a condom." She withdrew her hand. I explained my purpose. She congratulated me on my intelligence and responsibility. We praised each other for being so sensible. In the course of this mutual admiration session, Caroline reinstated her right hand on my penis and added the other, as one might when wishing to convey strong fellow-feeling on comforting the bereaved.

After a short pause, she produced a condom from somewhere about her person. "Come," said Caroline. She applied the condom, stripped off a garment or two and we engaged immediately. "Slowly," she cautioned, although she herself was hurrying the process, "I am small." She eased me in, making slight gasping noises—whether genuine or for effect, I could not tell. Whatever the case, she came rapidly to a climax, her legs and arms clasped tightly over my back. "Wait," she said, and slowed my movements, bringing down her legs and closing them under me. "Come on then," she commanded, and appeared to have another orgasm. "Do what you like now," she then conceded and so, having pleasured her, I took my own pleasure and concluded our commercial "act of love".

Caroline rinsed and dressed, then recommenced massaging me; much more vigorously this second time round, as if stimulated by the intercourse. "How good is business?" I asked. "Alright," she replied, and rattled away cheerfully about customers and tips. "The desk takes most of my fee as protection money," she said, "so I depend on tips." I assumed that she meant the woman at the reception desk would not allocate her clients unless she got a cut in advance.

"Most men are generous," she carried on, "even if I do not give them a special, they give me a tip." She named a sum about the equivalent of twenty American dollars. "For specials, of course, the usual." Caroline's 'specials' were not very special at all—almost the rule, it seemed. Most massage women were coy about how much full sex they had, but Caroline more or less admitted to a norm of at least a couple a day, assuming that she was getting her fair share of customers in good times.

Caroline was frank about earning most of her money through

her amiable and often enthusiastic prostitution. She commented just as explicitly on the range of masculine virility and the size and consistency of organs. Fat men tended to have small penises, while those smaller or comparatively athletic were more generously endowed. A long penis when flaccid might promise much (including alarm to its intended recipient), but often the owner failed to erect it beyond a certain soft engorgement. Small penises, on the other hand, could expand disproportionately into relatively large, hard organs, she noted.

Caroline's centre was located deep inside what she termed a family hotel, which gave the massage women some security both against the anti-vice authorities and the rougher or more drunken element among their potential clientele. Despite the domestic atmosphere there, she was occasionally called to a hotel room where proceedings were totally safe from outsiders or time limits and could be quite prolonged.

She recounted one such experience with an old New Zealander of eighty-nine. Concerned that she might break his ancient bones, she treated him lightly until he scolded her for her half-heartedness. "Let me massage you," he said and so she submitted to his attentions, which proved very robust. It seemed he had been a chiropractor or an osteopath. "You're a nice girl," he said and gave her an enormous tip: two hundred American dollars. "He was a nice old man," she echoed, casually adding that he was incapable of an erection.

At the other end of the age scale, Caroline recalled having serviced spoilt-brat teenagers, children of rich men who were inclined to let their male offspring do as they pleased in the purchase of sex. The youngest in this category was seventeen, an Indian national who claimed he had his first sex at eleven. Caroline was not greatly enamoured of intercourse with young men as they tended to be hasty and force themselves into her before she was properly aroused, despite the lady's own rapid approach. Once or twice, a father-and-son team had visited the centre, though they did not patronise the same woman. Sometimes, a man whose wife and family were staying in the hotel would pop in for a quick one: appointment, intercourse, clean-up and tip all over within ten minutes.

I asked Caroline for examples of violence or criminality that she had experienced in her profession. She replied that she had had an unpleasant encounter with a Japanese who insisted on having sex without a condom. "Oh no," Caroline said, whereupon the Japanese threatened to violate her willy-nilly, claiming that he was a gangster in order to make her more inclined to submit. Caroline exited the cubicle fast and sought the help of the receptionist. The Japanese followed her and banged his fist on the reception desk, which the two women were soon cowering behind. Eventually, they called hotel security and the man was escorted out, still threatening all and sundry with the wrath of the mafia.

Another Japanese subsequently informed Caroline that no respectable Japanese gangster would ever admit to being a gangster—at least not in such a vulgar manner. He knew this because, he modestly conceded, he was a bona fide gangster himself. His penis contained three or four hard little lumps of jade, or some such semi-precious material, inserted to give

189

greater pleasure to the fortunate women that he deigned to copulate with. Apparently, they were also an indication of *rank*, so a super-gangster would be permitted up to ten. I expressed some incredulity at all this, but Caroline said that she could feel the little lumps both with her fingers and her vagina.

Caroline herself had a medium-sized tattoo, a butterfly, her trade-mark, strategically located around the upper area of her protuberant little rump. The butterfly's abdomen thus fused with her rear cleavage and its wings spread a good six centimetres on either side. This decoration was presented as an aesthetic bonus to her customer's gaze if he were approaching its owner from behind. I found this feature engaging; as, indeed, I found much of Caroline.

The greatest reward that Caroline had ever enjoyed came not from a member of the mafia, but from a young, indecently rich pawn-shop owner. I thought at first she was referring to a pornographer and wondered where in Singapore such an enterprise could make its owner a fortune. But this client obtained his money more ruthlessly than by peddling pictures— extracting money from the impoverished or the desperate or the improvidential by charging usurious interest, illustrating that greed is more harmful than lust.

Certainly, he had money to throw around as he gave Caroline thirteen hundred American dollars for one session. I asked Caroline if this was generosity or a form of sexual exhibitionism. She did not understand my question, but described her reaction —which was mostly alarm. She feared she might be accused of theft if such a large sum were found on her. To allay her panic or conscience, she treated all the women in the centre to a meal and gave them a share of what was left—including even the rapacious lady at the reception desk.

I myself considered the pawn-shop owner's generosity a form of sexual showing-off. I liked to reward the massage women with tips over and above their usual fees for their specials, however. I warmed to them and their vulnerability and, if they were not greedy or pushy, which was only rarely the case, showed my appreciation of their moderation and pleasantness with some generosity.

Of course, the purchase of sex carries an inherent stimulus in itself, an addition to the idea of possession. The pawn-shop owner was doubtless indulging himself in an expression of power. He could take what he wanted and give what he wanted and enslave Caroline to his will—or so he thought. For he subsequently offered her ten thousand American dollars to find him a virgin for his personal use. He told her how he had once purchased a maiden by putting up her entire family, mother and father included, in an expensive hotel, paying for the finest meals they could eat. The virgin was duly bedded, deflowered and returned to her family. The parents received their thousands of dollars for the single night.

Even pragmatic Caroline was shocked at this heartlessness. But wealth is power and money can make much acceptable. Doubtless, it was quite rational of the family, if poverty-stricken, to gain at least some security for the future in this time-honoured style of pandering to the sexual whims of the stinking rich. Caroline did not report this individual as cruel or repulsive, just ruthlessly opportunistic—and generous with it. Still, she made no attempt to oblige him with a second treat.

Fairly soon after I met her, Caroline moved to Malacca, initially to a centre, though she intended to leave this form of her trade and earn her living by acquiring and keeping a circle of a few favoured clients. She planned to set herself up as a small independent business, offering massage and sex in small hotels or on holiday weekends elsewhere.

I soon lost touch with Caroline as I had not visited her that often and, although warm and generous by nature, she was not sentimental about her commercial arrangements. Experience had taught her that kindness and consideration were productive and helped her in her profession, as in many services, but that feelings other than friendship were best avoided in the twilight world.

Speedo Dream

Jonathan Lim

in tight blue speedos
the dream came
a midnight shape promising dark delights
curves pronounced and pronouncing
sweeping me into their shadows
i watch him walk in those trunks
and feel the tightness around me
my heart
and my groin
i could not breathe
air whispered thinly around me
whispered sins that sounded like heaven
the rest of him
bared
browned
brawn
briny from the sea
i longed to lick the salt off that skin
coat the smoothness with mine

but my eyes are drawn mercilessly
to that passion-blue bulge of wet
i could feel it under my hand
almost
the damp slick textured thrill
synthetic fibre over perfect flesh
tight fabric stretched over tighter things
so much pleasure squeezed
into such a space
i want to set it free
from the skimpy attempt at decency
why hide what is undisguisable
there is truth in there
beyond words
that only flesh knows
i would know your truth
i feel i almost know it already
let me into your glory
that sanctuary framed in flesh
where i may worship
and lose myself in my speedo dream

Femme Fatale

O Thiam Chin

Revenge was topmost on Pearlyn's mind as she entered the master bedroom. She had done a quick headcount of the number of people in today's sex group. Eight men, five women. Thirteen, a good number—and ironical too, she thought, chuckling to herself.

As the men and women single-filed into the bedroom, small talk and suppressed whispers continued to be exchanged. One of the men, the owner of this five-room flat in Jurong, had switched on the CD player and a soft, ethereal tune began to play. The bedroom smelled of cheap aromatherapy oils, and several stubs of candles were lighted around the room, throwing waving, elongated human shadows on the walls. The thick, velvety curtains had been drawn shut. Pearlyn hated the pervasive aromatherapeutic smell that plagued the room, but she chose to grin and bear the odours silently.

The men were the first to take off their clothes, dropping their pants and removing their light-coloured polo-tees or long-sleeved shirts in a haste, impatient to start the session. The women, on the other hand, fumbled with their tight skirts and bra-straps. A few eager men even assisted some of the women with their undressing.

Pearlyn took her time as she undressed, wanting to seize the opportunity to focus the lusty eyes of the men in the bedroom on her. She knew her body well enough to use it to its advantages—her smooth, slender legs, her 36D-sized breasts, and her shaved pussy. It was the latter asset, that shaved pussy, that turned the men on; she knew men were attracted by it, its bareness conveying a sense of vulnerability and virginity that drew men to it. Pearlyn had concluded this with a cold, hard clarity from the numerous group-sex sessions she had attended in the past few months.

The ruttish men wasted no time as they moved in on the women in the group they wanted. A young muscle-clad man approached Pearlyn and began to fondle her breasts gently. Pearlyn moaned in response and arched her body forward, pushing it towards him. "You are number one," she muttered inwardly.

The young man took her hands and guided her to a sheep-skin rug beside the large bed and lay her on it. Spreading her legs, Pearlyn pressed the man's head to her chest; the man began to nibble at her hardened nipples. Pearlyn let out a louder groan this time, drawing other available men, unknowing victims, to her web.

She closed her eyes and receded into her secret thoughts, like an elusive sea creature slipping into a deeper, darker depth. The young man jerked her body upwards as he lay on his back, and in this sitting position, Pearlyn guided his hard cock into her, edging it in roughly, causing the man to take a harder bite on her left breast. Another man approached from behind and pushed himself into her ass. Number two, she counted.

Her time would soon be up, Pearlyn knew, but before she went, she would take as many of them with her as possible, like an ancient Egyptian pharoah who brought his whole household, family and slaves, with him when he passed into the next world.

Pearlyn had received the news nine months ago, when she went for an anonymous AIDS test at Kelantan Lane, a month after a particularly hot-and-heavy session when the guy who had doggie-fucked her broke his condom. Completely devastated by the results, she took a free-fall into an emotional chasm. She wrestled through the whole gamut of experiences, from denial and anger to what-ifs and what-could-have-beens. But one thing that she had refused to come to terms with was acceptance. She refused to back down in the face of death. She had never been a victim, and she refused, even now with this disease, to become a victim.

The only residue from this exhausting existential struggle, after all her emotion, physical strength and will-power were spent, was the deep, bone-dry anger that left an indelible mark on her. This anger soon hardened into a rage that simmered menacingly under her nonchalant façade. And it was this intense rage that gave her back the will to live, to do what she had set her mind to achieve: this plan of revenge, claiming her pound of flesh.

Pulling herself away from the *ménage à trois*, Pearlyn moved on to the small cluster on the bed, their arms and legs all over one another. She grabbed a purplish-looking cock brusquely from another woman and roughly nudged her aside. She began to suck on it hungrily before inserting it into her. She started to pump away, deeper and deeper, and groaned ecstatically with every thrust. Another down, she noted.

So from one man to another, to another, Pearlyn moved among the group of sweaty bodies with a profound determination, making mental notes on who had been exposed and who still hadn't. Her mind was sharp and her body flushed red from the physical exertions.

Finally, the session wound down to an end, as people started to break away from the action and began cleaning themselves with handfuls of Kleenex and wet tissues. Pearlyn got off the bed, her body shining like a new-born Venus emerging from a giant shell, glistering in the dimness of the room with tiny droplets of cum and perspiration. She moved to the pile of clothes on the floor, picked up her white cotton shirt and silk pleated skirt, and, without wiping herself off, began to put on her clothes. Her white shirt plastered itself to her chest and back, making it almost translucent.

Once she was done, Pearlyn left the master bedroom quietly and went into the living room where she collected her black Gucci bag from the couch. With a quick check on its contents, and a backward glance and snicker at the bedroom, she left the apartment.

As Pearlyn was about to enter the lift, she dug out her PDA from the bag and flicked it on. Checking through her calendar, she noted that there would be another session this coming Saturday at 7 pm, at an executive condominium in Bishan. "Good," she uttered softly under her breath, her eyes glistening brightly, with an almost inhuman intensity.

By The Time

Jonathan Lim

by the time he said
would I
the breath held, caught in his heart
trembling with the echo of words still unsaid
soon to be

by the time he said
can I
my lips matte-dry
tensed midway between a smile and another just waiting

by the time he asked
may I
my eyes tingling with the probe
searching his eyes for secrets to claim
to conquer

by the time he asked
I already had

Beige Walls
And Floral Sheets

Samarah Zafirah

5 pm

The yellow blush that peers shyly behind the sullen concrete
structures breaks through the organza pink curtains, scattering
orange streaks against your brown skin, like lashes from a leather
whip. But the heat could not pierce your body. Nor could the
shrieks of scrambling bikes weaving precariously through traffic,
making jagged stitches with trails of smoke against the asphalt.
Drivers honk expletives at each other as though the journey home
were responsible for their depression. The heavier public buses
haul their overloaded cargo on stretched rubber wheels, hissing
through the neighbourhood, annoying half-deaf grannies trying
to nap before the return of their clamouring grandchildren. But
you remain undisturbed, unmoving except for the ebb and flow
of your breath, oblivious to the colours of sound and light.

I catch a glimpse of beauty in your sleep. Propping my body
to one side, I trace the undulating terrain of yours. Your lips,
slightly parted, speak of the gratitude brought by relinquished

inhibitions: how a while ago you had stripped me bare and beckoned me to the centre of the bed with a slap on the pillow. Then you, too, had left all possible thread on your body sprawling on the floor, as if feeding them to cotton-eating pigeons. Subtly, you had slipped my thigh between your thighs, warm and wet as I raised my knee and buried my heel deep into the mattress. Your lips travelled the length of my body like footprints on forbidden ground, each imprint made with caution and in anticipation of a greater conquest. My lips, parted, were gagged by the pleasure that the intrusive finger and evasive tongue double-knotted. A scream, begun but quickly restrained, created ripples that spread across my body. My thighs pressed themselves against each other and my nipples surrendered to the currents of the flesh. My eyes denied the persistent presence of the real world that you and I reside in. They hated to see the beige walls and floral sheets that would mark the end of this calm.

You kissed my lips. On them, I tasted the residue of the untamed sea and braced myself for another type of voyage.

Your face, now half-buried in the pillow, is warm from the orange glow that penetrates the room. Your shoulder, rounded and smooth but laden with the heart's wild terrain, is now weightless. Your arms are bent one over the other like a pair of scissors, as wrist meets wrist. These arms, like reins across your chest, tame the breasts that had earlier hung wildly as my thigh's saddle whetted your desire. Your thighs, adorned with streaks of gold, are like prison bars trapping you in time.

You snuggle against my chest, embarrassed that sleep is a reward for bliss. I run my fingers through your hair and plant a kiss on it, as if to tell you how much I have enjoyed watching you sleep, unabashed.

Time has never been a friend at this hour. Time would eventually jolt you from sleep and steal a heartbeat. Soon, the room will turn dark; the orange fades into a sinister blue, then black. The final cries of birds will bring jitters to our unwrapped bodies, every tinkle a potential threat — the bicycle's chime, the neighbour's door bell, the salesman's persistence. We will smile as you clumsily help me with the hooks and eyes of the garment that covers my modesty, mindful that any accidental brush can cause a shudder. We will laugh at the tricks our ears play with invaded keyholes and swinging doors, but only after our gasps of fear dissipate. Then our fingers will scurry through button holes, belt holes, watches and rings, while our eyes keep pace with the mocking second hand.

6.30 pm

We curse the familiar floral sheets and beige walls with silence before we leave the room. Our euphoria is over. Time has won again.

The Phoenix Tattoos

Richard Lord

It was probably because he was at Spinelli's that day. He was really a Coffee Bean person. His drink was cappuccino, and neither Spinelli's nor Starbucks has the right cup for cappuccino. Their cups are all tall and thin, so you get all the milk and foam at once and only reach the coffee when you near the end of your drink.

For that reason alone, he rarely went to Spinelli's. And, deeply addicted to habit, he hated altering his routine. Strange, unwelcome things often happened to him when he broke routine. Which may be why on that day, having gone to Spinelli's for his cappuccino, he had that "episode."

While manoeuvering the cup so that he could draw a good swallow of coffee along with the thick clouds of foam, he happened to look over and noticed her. She was pretty, of course, but so were many of the other girls sitting there, or walking by, some much prettier. But his eyes locked on this one. Wait a minute, wasn't she …? No, that wasn't her, but … suddenly, it came back to him, at least a part of it. That one time. The two of them together, and fantastic sex.

He couldn't remember her name, or where he had met her,

even where they had gone to make love ... well, have sex. It couldn't really have been love. It was more like ... Like?

No, none of that came back to him; but the lovemaking was indelibly printed on his brain. As he gazed at her across the room, he recalled that so pale body, every lovely contour: the smallish but well-shaped breasts, the low sweep of her back proceeding up in a gentle slope to her buttocks, the dark wedge of hair between her thighs.

Just as he started considering that it might have been simply a dream that this girl had turned up in—maybe he had once seen her on the street or in a mall and his flash craving for her returned in a dream—she looked up. The expression on her face, stun and bitterness together, told him it was not just a dream; she *had* been there, wherever it was. His eyes and brow scrunched up, as if to ask her where they knew each other from. But she instantly turned away, looked around for another table and, not finding one in the crowded café, simply pivoted her chair so her back was to him.

He kept staring, however, and on seeing her back, that other key detail suddenly flashed. Yes, how could he have ever forgotten that? The phoenix tattoo, double-headed, there on the small of her back, on the left side. Hypnotic. In such vibrant colours it seemed to be dancing slowly in its flames, even as she lay absolutely still. And it had an identical twin on the crown of her right breast.

Yes, the two tattoos. The thing was, they weren't just adornments: they played such an important role in their lovemaking. By just pressing them, he could make her instantly aroused, or intensify the pleasure. On that day—or evening, or whenever—when they had been together, he would lean forward during the coupling and kiss the tattoo on her breast while gently pressing the other on her back. She'd start to climax, and he would press harder on the one tattoo while kissing the breast tattoo more intensely. She would come, screaming, digging the blunt side of her fingers into his neck, then drag them down his back, pull at his hair with her teeth, maybe bite his neck or ear as he lifted his head from her breast.

All of this he could remember so acutely. Yet nothing else.

She was waiting for someone, a friend apparently, and that second girl arrived within minutes. She must have told this friend about the episode, because after a short, heads-lowered exchange, the friend looked up and floated him a dirty look. Hell, he must have done something terrible at the time—but he hadn't the slightest inkling of what it was.

He couldn't keep from staring over at them, so he edged his chair sideways, in the other direction, and tried to busy himself. But this whole thing was beginning to gnaw further inside him, upsetting the carefully arranged furniture of habit and planning. Nothing like this had ever happened to him, that some details of such an incident remained so vivid—he could see, hear, even taste them right there—and that he completely forgot other details at least as important.

He pulled out a notebook, found a clean page and started sketching the tattoo. As he drew, he recalled how just kissing the tattoo on her lower back had brought her to fierce arousal, how her legs would thrash and her butt gyrate as he kissed her there again and again, his lips and tongue pressing into her pliant flesh.

He pulled out a red pen to add more colour, more "activity" to his drawing. He only had the black and the red, while the tattoos themselves flaunted other rich colours: ochre, green, gold, purple ... one he couldn't even name. But he was able to come up with a good facsimile, considering his meagre materials. He smiled: yeah, not at all bad. Maybe he should have listened to less practical people and gone into graphic art instead of law. He would certainly not have made as much money as he did now, but he might actually be happier.

When he finished, he turned back and looked over to their table. They were still talking, this time ignoring him. He added a few last strokes to the drawing; yes, that's pretty close to the way it looked. He glanced over at them again. Even from this angle, he could see how alluring the girl was. The way her shift pulled against her body as she sat in the chair made him think of that same body naked, writhing there in the bed against the moist, pink sheets. Wherever it had taken place.

He closed the notebook, finished his cappuccino in one long gulp and thought of just leaving, taking a wide turn away from them as he exited. Almost immediately, however, he realised this was impossible. How could he walk away from this woman with whom he had apparently shared something incredible, yet lost so much of. He *had to* find out what this was all about, or at least make more of an attempt than that feeble questioning look he had thrown her.

He pulled out the notebook again, carefully tore out the

page with the drawing, rose and moved quickly over to their table. The friend looked up first; the girl herself gave him just a cursory glance, turned, looked down and started twisting the edges of a serviette into tiny cones. "Could you please get out of here? We're having a conversation, in case you didn't notice."

"Actually, I did notice," he replied. "But I wanted to give you something." He placed the drawing down on the table, right in front of the girl. Her friend looked puzzled. The girl turned to her friend and said something in a soft voice; he tried, but was unable to make out more than a few words. The friend nodded, stood up, started moving away. About a metre from the table, she spun around and pointed to her watch.

"Fifteen minutes," the girl said, shaking her head, then turned back to him. "Okay, you can sit down if you like." He nodded, pulled out the nearest chair to hers and started to slide it a little closer. "Not there," she snapped. "Take that one," pointing to the chair on the opposite side of the table. He shrugged and settled himself into that seat.

She picked up the drawing and stared at it. Her face indicated that she was impressed. "That's your tattoo, isn't it?" She nodded. "You have it here," he pointed to the spot on his own back; she nodded again. "And the other one ... higher up, on the other side."

She looked at him fully for the first time since she had first spotted him. "Yes, so what?"

He shifted uneasily, but allowed himself to place his hands on the table.

"Do you know who I am?" He tried to control his voice, to

sound calm, but a slight note of desperation slipped in.

"Of course. What do you think, that I'd forget something like that? Shit, you have an even lower opinion of me than I thought."

"No, no, it's not that, it's just … Alright, now how can I explain this?" He searched for the next path to follow. "Do you know my name?"

She snorted out a derisive laugh. "No, I don't. You didn't want to tell me, remember? You said, 'Just call me David Beckham.'"

"No, I don't remember, that's the problem. I just don't … I mean, there are so many details there from that … time together. So vivid up here." He pointed to his head. "But then so much I just can't recall."

"Like?"

"Like … just your name. Did you tell me your name?"

"Of course, I did. I guess I was just too naïve back then. I trusted guys."

He felt a surge of free-floating guilt. Yes, he probably had treated her terribly. That may be why he was experiencing this bout of selective amnesia. He'd read somewhere how the brain often filters out things that are especially unpleasant, or that we're horribly ashamed of. A defence mechanism that helps us to move on. But what horrible thing could he have done? She didn't seem to bear any traces of physical damage. What could he have done to her inside?

"*Any*-thing else?" She snapped his contemplation with the harshness of this question.

"Yeah: a lot else. Where did it happen? Here in Singapore? At your place, at the uni hostel, a friend's? Or were we somewhere on holiday?"

She stung him with a look that said such an insulting question deserved only dire contempt. She turned, the bitter look still on her face, to check a message on her handphone. "I have to go," she said icily without bothering to turn back to him.

But he couldn't let it end there. "I'm sorry, but this has never happened to me before. Hey, I'm only twenty-seven. I usually get praised for my good memory. But I really can't remember too much about that time we were ... together. Just the ... well, the mechanics really and ... your tattoos. Those tattoos were like some hypnotic medallions."

"I see, so all you remember is the sex? Getting inside me, pumping like crazy, the stormy kisses, all that. Pushing all the right buttons, pulling all the right cords. Isn't that what you guys call it?"

"Well, I also remember the colour of the sheets; they were pink, right? And that ugly bedside lamp ... then there was this thin rug which was a horrendous shade of green, and ..." He looked up; it had suddenly come back to him. "And you said you would take me the next day to where you got your tattoos." She said nothing, didn't nod, but her narrowed eyes told him he was right. "You said you wanted me to get two just like them. You said it was ... necessary, that it was part of our being together."

"So you don't forget everything. You have a good memory for what you want to remember."

"I want to remember it all. I want to remember your name, where we were, why we were there, how we got that far ..." He stopped, suddenly realising that he had swept past what could be the key to the whole episode. "And ... why didn't I go and get the tattoos?"

Her eyes narrowed further, as if they were turning into small creatures—mythical beings, half-reptile, half-whatever—going into attack mode. He actually started to get scared, thinking she might be able to physically attack him, take revenge for some wrong that he couldn't remember but deeply deserved to be punished for.

"The pact," she whispered, and then smiled. The smile looked like it tasted of strychnine. But it seemed as if this was a taste she enjoyed.

Here, he closed his own eyes, tightly. For one thing, he didn't want to see her face at this moment. But more importantly, he needed to dig deep within himself to recover what kind of pact they could have made. If it was still there, he would find it. Nothing. He opened his eyes again, slowly, half-believing she'd be gone when he looked. But she was still there, of course. However, the smile was gone; this time, there were tears trickling down her cheeks. As they reached her mouth, she opened it slightly and eased her tongue out. It seemed like she wanted to swallow them, to wash the acrid taste from her mouth.

"I'm sorry, I just can't ... what *pact* was this?"

She closed her mouth tightly, her stare fixed on him, and the tears seemed to stop instantly. "Look, I'm *really* sorry if I've upset you. I didn't mean that at all. I just wanted to ... to get the whole story on what happened there."

"There's no story," she answered. "There's just ways in and ways out." She glanced again at her handphone, more as an excuse than to read any messages there. "I have to go."

She stood, started pulling her shopping bags together, then turned slightly to grab something off the next chair. Only at that moment did the impulse seize him; he acted on it without hesitation. As she was turned slightly to the right, he lunged over and touched the spot where he thought he remembered the tattoo being. He was, as it were, spot on. At the initial touch, she stiffened. As he pressed harder against her flesh, she gasped. Her face knotted in a look of unwanted arousal. But almost immediately, she recovered: she swung around, looking like she had just been bitten by a snake. The expression on her face now clearly warned she was quite ready to attack.

What the hell was he doing? He could be charged with outrage of modesty. He was a lawyer, he knew that. If convicted, he could be suspended from practicing law—for years maybe.

But being a lawyer, he also knew that he had a ready defence. He was just reaching out to flick something off her shift, there on the back. How did this constitute a sexual assault? To prove his guilt, she'd have to prove some offence was actually committed. Boy, would he love to see this in court: for her to stand up, expose the tattoo, have a deputy prosecutor touch the spot and watch her soar into instant ecstasy. The judge might even ask if he could touch it himself, just to be certain. He knew a few who would probably insist. He laughed at this notion.

Of course, she had no idea he was laughing at some imagined

judge, not her. So when she slapped him hard and jolted the laugh from his face, he was not, as he could have been, riled. But he realised it was useless trying to explain the matter to her. He would just accept the slap as a down payment on what he probably deserved from her.

"A joke, is it? Everything's a joke for you." She clutched her bags again and looked ready to pivot and leave.

"No, it's not a joke, not at all. Look, stay just five more minutes. I'm ready to fulfill my side of the pact. But I don't remember what it is. Honestly." She looked at him hard, in a way he couldn't read. Was she trying to judge whether to believe him or not? Or was she waiting for the perfect moment to do something awful to him, to gain what she must see as her justified revenge? "Honestly," he repeated. "Honestly." He shook his head in frustration, aware of how deeply dishonest the word "honestly" can sound.

Her features softened significantly. Had he reached her? Was she willing to listen to him, to give him back those parts of the story he was missing? Or was this just a trick to lull him before she struck again? She said nothing for about a minute, just stared at him; he felt like a cord was twisting inside him, slowly pulling his throat down further into his chest.

"No, I really have to go. I do." She reached down, picked up a sheet of paper from the table, slightly torn at the top, coffee stains at one edge. She held it out to him. "This is yours."

"No, you can keep it. It's ... it's a present."

She smiled at him for the first time, a smile without the strychnine anyway. She then reached into her soft black bag, extracted a pen, and inscribed something on the sheet. She extended it to him once more. "Now it's my present to you." After a slight hesitation, he took the drawing back.

"I have to go."

"Can you give me a number or something where I can contact you?"

"No. You can't contact me."

"Okay then, how about ... at least tell me where was it? Where did we? No, better, why are those tattoos so ... so powerful?"

She smiled again, more warmly this time, whispered, "It's there," turned and moved off quickly. He rose, but then just stood there, watching her go. Until she disappeared, he had almost forgotten that he was holding the drawing. He quickly looked to see what she had written. He read, "What you can touch is just the beginning of what you can feel."

He frowned, then folded the sheet in half and slipped it into his wallet, next to the credit cards. "The beginning of what you can feel?" Well, he should be able to work this one out. He was a lawyer after all, someone who used logic to herd and corral the irrational.

And what was that last thing she said? "It's there?" What's there? The secret of the tattoos, the place where they met, the reason she couldn't tell him?

Hmm ... it was like his cappuccino, probably: at the bottom of all the foam, all the clouds, you eventually found what you were looking for. As she said, it's there. And, somehow, he knew that it was.

Every Other Man

Cyril Wong

A few days after Robert decided he would come out of the closet, he discovered the parks where men like him hung out in wait for each other. The experience proved exhilarating for all of four encounters with sad, expressionless men who seemed all hungry mouths and hands. He decided to try out the pubs next.

One evening, he wandered into a Karaoke pub and ended up being fondled by an Australian tourist in one of the private rooms. Each room had a small coffee table, a curved sofa and a television with cheap microphones. First, they took turns singing. The guy told Robert he had a nice voice. Then they unzipped and sucked each other off on the sofa that smelled of beer and cigarettes. The Australian was not very good at carrying a tune nor otherwise.

On another occasion, Robert met a car salesman in another bar who destroyed a Cantonese love song while swivelling restlessly from side to side on his stool. He caught Robert cringing and came over to confess he was slightly tone-deaf. Robert neither agreed nor disagreed. He bought Robert a drink. They talked till they were asked to leave by the Eurasian bartender who, both agreed, was very handsome.

After dating for a week, both said *I love you* to each other at the end of every telephone conversation. They had sex on weekends at the salesman's place, but only when his aged parents were already asleep in the next room. Robert liked that his lover's penis was long and not too thick. He only found it disturbing that when the salesman moaned, it reminded him of his own father, who made such a sound once when he had a high fever and struggled to sleep at night.

The sound also reminded him that his father had stopped talking to him twenty years earlier after discovering him one morning in bed with another man. The next morning, after their night of lovemaking, Robert and the salesman talked about renting an apartment and moving in with each other one day.

The same week, Robert met all of the salesman's closest friends. One of them heard Robert sing at a Karaoke club that had just opened. He asked if Robert wanted to be the lead for his band that played late-80's pop songs at a café owned by a Christian businessman who was secretly bisexual. Robert said yes. The salesman started coming to the cafe every evening after work just to hear him sing.

A month later, the salesman left for a business trip and never came back. His friends told Robert that he must have found a better job, or even a new man. The night that Robert decided he was no longer in love with the salesman, one of the other band members asked him to come over to his place for a drink. Both of them got really drunk and started to make out. Robert almost cried when he discovered the guy had a smaller penis than he had hoped.

They tried to get it on, but Robert could not get the salesman out of his mind. Neither of them could sustain an erection, despite the energy spent trying to arouse each other. As Robert's thighs were being lacquered by the other man's tongue, his mind drifted to a scene in the café where the salesman was sitting at the table he always occupied to watch Robert perform.

He would smile brightly whenever their eyes met over the heads of other people, or he would be nodding to a steady, encouraging rhythm that was not at all in time with the music. Suddenly, the salesman's face began to blur, to become his father's face. Then it slowly blurred to become the face of every other man that he had ever dated. Maybe it was the alcohol, the moon suspended in the sky like a dirty bulb outside the window, or the fact that the man who had been trying for the last half-hour to turn him on had given up and fallen asleep on his stomach, but for some strange and unknowable reason, Robert seriously wished that he could close his eyes, take a long deep breath ... and die. He closed his eyes. He took the deepest breath he had ever taken, and nothing happened.

A Spy In The House

Chris Mooney-Singh

It is March, 1986. I am Peter and I am eight years old. Yes, I can remember everything clearly.

"You are my man," says Mummy. "I love you, I love you, I love you," squashing my mouth and cheeks in her hands as she kisses me and goes off for mahjong at Mei Li Auntie's.

Imelda is doing the ironing. She sings a song, about a man outside a lady's window. We sing it together at the end of each verse. *Come down, lady, come down.*

Daddy returns home from the office, putting his big silver case on the table. He is a salesman.

"Peter," Daddy says and picks me up and tosses me higher up toward the fan, but not that high, but I still squeal like a piglet. I don't like it. I start crying. Daddy laughs. Sometimes he can look really hard and mean and keeps waggling me up there with his strong hands.

Imelda is in the kitchen, taking out the covered dishes to put on the living room table. Rice, fish, *taugay* and *sambal*.

"Give me. I'll take him."

I'm wriggling like a fish from one set of hands into another. It's time for my afternoon nap, but I fight and kick.

"Peter! Do what she says!" he shouts. He sits down to eat lunch.

Imelda gets a hold of me and carries me off to my bedroom over her shoulder like a bag of rice from the market. She dumps me on the bed.

"Now be good, my little slippery mackerel," she says, fluffing the pillow around my head. "You will sleep, okay. All the way to the island where Grandfather Pablo has his fishing boat."

She sits down and strokes my forehead and then runs her hand over my body, touching my wee-wee and I begin to calm down. Soon I'm drifting off faraway across the sea to the island where fishermen are pulling the net and the fish are cascading coins in the moonlight and the man is singing below the window *Come down, lady, come down ...*

I wake up. It is hot. I go to the kitchen. "Melda!" I try to say, but my tongue is a dried strip of jackfruit. My voice comes out like a transistor radio with nearly-dead batteries. No answer. I go to the sink and fill up a glass with water from the tap and drink.

The house is quiet. I go to my parents' room. No one there. I go back to the living room. Then I see Daddy's silver case, still on the table. I climb up, because he is not around and I want to see what is in there. For once. I click the locks open and lift the lid. There are some files, a calculator, writing pad, books and, down at the bottom, two or three magazines. They all have pictures of ladies on them.

I pick one up and flick through until I come to the centre part. Same lady. Different shots. Not wearing any clothes, but wearing black-rimmed glasses. She is on the bed, knees gathered to her white belly, reading a book, her hair tied in a bun. Another: stretched out with a writing pad, holding a pen in her hand, open study books spread around on the bed, pink nipples peeping through her long hair.

I can't figure it out. Shame, shame! Why does she not have any clothes on? She's not in the bathtub. I turn the page. The same girl. This time she is wearing a flat black hat just like my big cousin Won Shu wearing his black hat when he finished studying and got that rolled-up paper placed in his hand on the stage. There is a calendar printed in one corner and she's wearing a blue sweater, cradling books and holding up a red apple, while the other hand is lifting the short skirt. I snigger. She hasn't got panties on and is showing her wee-wee that's black and hairy just like Imelda's in the shower sometimes when she lets me come in. I can't figure it out. It doesn't make sense at all! I dump the magazine inside and click the locks of the silver case closed and get down from the chair.

Where is everybody? It's all very strange. I call out again "Melda!" Nothing. She must be taking a nap also. I scamper down the long hall to the back door. I hear loud music on the radio. She is playing it in the maid quarters, outside in the back part of our house. I put my ear to the door. Along with the music I can hear some other sounds. Sort of like a piglet, but different. Is she hurt? I go round the other side and peep through the iron-grill window with its glass shutters open for air. The white curtain is blowing as the overhead fan turns. The music is louder now. Imelda and Daddy are on the bed. They don't have any clothes on. Playing. Sort of like the magazine. I don't understand. She is underneath, her legs up in the air. Daddy is holding her, and his wee-wee is now a red stick thing which he is sticking into her wee-wee. Sometimes mine has gone like that when Imelda helps me go to sleep. Once it went all hard. She laughed and gave it a little kiss, singing "One day, darling, one day ..."

Daddy is now pushing hard between her legs, back and forth. She is making her little piglet grunts and squeals and getting louder and louder. He is groaning and laughing like a demon. She is now squealing very loud. Is he hurting her? I'm scared for her, but I'm more scared of him. Daddy can hit hard and I don't like it. Now she is really loud and him too, and suddenly he pulls out his thing and he is forcing it into her mouth. She gets up, kneels and starts sucking and helping with her hands, until he, too, is groaning and then lets out a final grunt as he pees white stuff all over her face and breasts. I can't figure any of this out, but I can't stop staring either. Finally, she flops on top of him with her head on his chest, toward me. It looks like they have gone to sleep, but then I notice her eyes are open. Staring. Then, she sees me. Imelda looks surprised, but then she changes and puts her finger to her lips, indicating not to make any sound at all. Which I don't.

I Didn't Expect
To Write About Sex

Cyril Wong

Did you know that after I came, I imagined my pelvis had emptied out into a dark cave you could crawl into, lay yourself down and fill my body with your sleep? This isn't really about sex, is it? Yet I could write about your tongue, how cleverly you rotated it like a key to slip open every lock of resistance under my skin, muscles loosening like a hundred doors creeping open across the conservative, suburban town of this flesh, desire stepping into the open like Meryl Streep in that film with Clint Eastwood, a wind calling forth the stiff body from under her dress so wholeheartedly how could she not help but undress, welcome it in. I could also write about your hands, tenacious dogs of your fingertips unearthing pleasure from every pore, jumpstarting nipples with the flick of your nails, each time you pushed in deeper from behind. I must not forget to write how much I love you when you warn me not to swallow; I love how I take you anyway into my mouth like tugging a recalcitrant child back into the house, even though he realizes deep inside himself that he would always long for home; I love how you taste, what was inside of you now inside of me, sliding down my throat like the sweetest secret. I could write about how when you fell off the peak of your mounting hunger, your hands stayed anchored upon my nape, as if to keep from drowning, as if to let me know, "Even when I'm this far gone, I'd want you here. I'd want you with me."

Celibation

Lee Yew Moon

I feel you come, just before I am about to release the tension that has pleasured me. Your lightness floats on me as you let go. Before I can come, you raise your hips and unsheathe my penis while the rest of you remains on me. You rock your hips and brush your pubic hair along my shaft, leaving moisture on me I will always smell.

Untamed, my penis tingles and strengthens. You peel slowly away from me.

Light floods between us. Dawn brings the squawk of a feral cockatoo which turns my face toward the window. The sky dazzles me. I turn back to look at you, and you are gone.

I'm still hard, throbbing ... but unfulfilled.

"So, you say this happens to you almost every morning?"

"Yes, Elder Anton."

"But we really have no proof that you are capable of ..." He paused, probably looking for words that would not offend. Offend his own value system, that is. "It's quite clear that you cannot get an erection. We have administered the three prescribed tests and it hasn't stood the test, so to speak."

"But Elder, I get it everyday, in the morning."

"So you say. But the council needs to see it. Our orders are very clear—when appropriately stimulated, candidates for elderhood must show ... arousal. Otherwise, as the Holy Chapters point out, the vow of chastity does not mean any sacrifice.'

"I know that, Elder." I was desperate. Yet I paused. "But why would I want to join your Order if I don't sense that I have been called? It isn't exactly a life of fun and games I am asking for."

There was a long pause. "The Inspired Ones were all-seeing. They knew that our Order could become the refuge of all manner of men hiding their inadequacies behind our restrictions and good repute."

Another pause.

"That's why we have the tests. On admission, all Elders must be fully functional men who have actively given up the enjoyment of those functions."

This was old ground.

"Yet it does not seem you are seeking refuge." He paused to look at me fully. 'And your earnestness is clearly deep. I will have to call the Council."

He trotted out of the Interview Room. About fifteen minutes passed. The door opened again. Elder Anton returned with another elder. They were, both of them, solemn.

"This is Elder Renee from the Seclusion Order. In matters such as these, we call on another Order to help us. As things are, we cannot admit you into our order. All three arousal tests have proven negative, and by this stage, all previous unqualified candidates have dropped out on their own."

The other elder spoke. "We're honestly very surprised that you're still so insistent on continuing. In fact, we are impressed." Short pause. "But we cannot let our impressions, strong though they may be, undermine the sacred laws of the Inspired Ones."

"I see." I got ready to leave.

"We took a closer look at the Holy Chapters, and discovered that while we cannot let our impressions decide your entry, we are allowed to give you one more chance if we are collectively of the opinion that the standard tests might have been unfair to you."

"The Council is of that opinion."

I stood naked in a room so dimly lit I could not even see its walls. I had been brought in blindfolded and told not to move beyond a chalk circle drawn on the floor. This was my last chance to join the Order, to prove that I could have an erection, even ejaculation, so that I could take a vow of chastity and truly abstain.

I waited until I tired and felt cold from my nakedness. I also tired because, once again, I had that … encounter … in my sleep. It woke me up even earlier than usual, and I did not sleep after that.

Being tired was not going to help, and I was not hopeful. Previous attempts had been well calibrated and I didn't know why I had not responded. The Order had tried to arouse me through visual, auditory, even smell stimuli. But I remained soft.

I tried very hard to invoke your presence to help me harden, but it only seemed to make matters worse!

A door opened and a faint glow filled the space. A female form, covered from head to toe in a white robe, came into view. She danced, with the grace of a ballerina. As she moved, her thin robe pressed against her otherwise naked form. Perhaps it was this, but also probably because I could smell her, that I sensed the fleeting touches of animal energy tingling my body. She danced around me, but just out of my reach. I could not keep my eyes off her.

There was no music! She danced, full of grace, to silence. Her robe parted to provide a glimpse of her pubis fettered only by a gentle bush. Her skin glowed amid the dimness. Her robe parted further to reveal her breasts heaving to her dance.

I reached out, but then remembered the chalk circle. I stretched out my hand and just managed to touch and hold her robe. It came off in my hand. Only her face remained covered.

Through her hood, our eyes met and I had to have her. I would break the rules and leave the circle; and, of course, the Order!

I dropped the robe and stepped out of the circle. She froze at my transgression. I reached out to touch her and saw her looking down. HELL! It was still ... soft. I was about to drag her into sex with me and I was still soft. I froze too. I looked up at her and noticed she was uncovering her head.

"Sister." It was Elder Anton. "Don't!"

"Sister?" I gasped. From the Seclusion Order? I felt sick. By then, she had run out of the room naked.

"As you can see for yourself, you have failed to achieve arousal." Elder Anton was agitated. "We cannot admit you into the Order. This has been your last chance. Please leave the room, dress and go. Do not come back to us again.'

It was then dark, and silent. I walked to where I felt the door was, opened it and started walking ...

... across twenty years into this room, beside her.

I don't know why I'd bothered. Since that day two decades ago, my only 'arousal' had been with you. I'd disappointed every other woman, even with medication. Ten years ago, I'd stopped trying or even responding.

When she poses at my figure-drawing classes, she puts her entire soul and body into the stillness of the pieces. My students love her for her beauty and ease, as do I.

Then she offers to show me her room. I accept, knowing she is 'safe'. So I am here.

After seeing her room, we chat. Our voices drift across the evening into the night—there seems much to chatter on about. It is almost morning and we are tired. She asks if she could lie down. I say it is her place. She asks if I'm tired, and if I'd do the same. There is only one bed.

The chatter floats and I fall asleep, preparing to meet you.

I am without clothes, and you are on top of me. You have slipped your vagina around my penis and are rubbing it with the gestures of sex. As you do so, you grip and let go of me, inducing a swell of pleasure, I also sense your pleasure.

I feel you come, just before I am about to release the tension that has pleasured me. Your lightness floats on me as you let go. I wait for you to raise your hips and unsheathe my penis ... but you go on. You rock your hips with me still inside and your scent, now mixed with mine, floods my senses.

You go on, and we thrash and thrash, and I move into a past when I had known pleasure.

I come, and come, and come.

Light floods between us. Dawn brings the squawk of a feral cockatoo which turns my face toward the window. The sky dazzles me. I turn back to look at you, and you are ... her!

"We ...?" You look at me, dripping with joy, wafting in our scent.

"Twenty years ago, I fell in love with you before I was born. I knew you would love me too, but you wanted to join that Order and I would have lost you forever. I had to keep you from that and from the other women, because I know you would have married them. I am sorry I made you wait so long."

We kiss.

What We Did Last Summer

Robert Yeo

For years, our London friend Sen had been enticing us to visit his "island".

"You'll love it. Everyone goes about wearing only a baseball cap or some kind of hat. Or, better still, nothing at all."

"Aiyoh," Eve exclaimed. At five foot two, she is my shorter and younger half, and at fifty-eight, she was in reasonable shape though she did not think so.

"That's all?" I asked.

"Well, you must apply sunblock and get the best because there is plenty of sun in summer in the south of France."

"Aiyah," Eve went on as as she felt that Sen had not responded to her first exclamation, "I am not in shape to go around naked at my age—"

"Who cares about age?" Sen remonstrated. "No one is going to ask how old you are. Anyway I'm sixty-five and Bob is the same age and you are younger."

Eve was silent, silenced by what Sen just said. "Besides, your name is Eve, right?"

I did not protest as I thought that growing up in Hougang in the forties and bathing in roadside taps had sufficiently prepared me for some kind of exposure. And yes, some years ago, back in 1990, a friend had dared me to bare all in Watson's Bay, off Sydney. The truth is that I had not adequately registered what it will mean to live in a naturist island in France. At sixty-six, bespectacled, a little paunchy, if I had thought a little more about it ... But perhaps my largely black locks may have lulled me into not thinking about my age, but thinking instead of the thrill of a new, nudist adventure. I had blue expectations, of the Mediterranean blue and of other kinds of blue ...

Sen, lean, tall and tanned, spoke from the confidence of having been there for more than three decades. His white, plentiful hair provided a contrast to his Anglo-Asian complexion. Now a Brit, the island was his annual escape. His retirement last year, and mine, the year before, had made this assignation possible. He was, at least, in shape as was his Asian-American girlfriend, a slim tall person with the figure of a model who did not look the forty-plus years she carried so lithely.

So, here we are, two senior citizens (though I don't know if he would welcome the dubious compliment) and a fifty plus woman, Asians, about to descend on his European island in the sun. The Ile du Levant, a half hour ferry ride from the coastal Riviera resort of Le Levandou, midway between the port of Toulon and St Tropez. In the height of summer, in the midst of the tourist season, Wednesday 3 August 2005, to be exact.

Arriving in the small pier, we saw a small bus waiting. "That's

Alain," Sen said, referring to the small, grizzled driver in shorts. The short ride uphill brought us to Eden Villas. "There's your paradise," Sen said to Eve. Our twin, en suite room had a queen-sized bed, cooking facilities and utensils and cost sixty euros per day. After settling down, we were introduced to two Englishwomen, Edith and Lesley, friends of Sen, who had taken the room next to his. Edith, a redhead, the older of the two appeared to be in her early fifties while Lesley was a fortyish blonde.

As soon as we had unpacked, Sen said it was time to go to the village square. Five o'clock and it was still hot and bright. All four emerged, wearing only a variety of hats, except for Les who decided to keep her knickers on. We soon got to talking animatedly; Eve and I had just met the two women and there was no trace of self-consciousness as we sauntered downhill. If I had imagined, before this, that I would be walking erect, if you know what I mean, well I did not. It was a good sign as it would have made walking very awkward.

The village square was a small paved space surrounded by three cafes with al fresco dining. We sat down, ordered our drinks and waited. Slowly, the place filled up. Sen received the most attention, as he was a regular while both Edith and Les, who had been there last year, bumped into returnees.

Bonjour Sen.

Bonjour Pierre.

Bonjour Edith.

Hello Gaston.

Effusive hugs and kisses on both cheeks. We were introduced

as neophytes. Men and women, whom I judged to be in their twenties and thirties, walked in the nude, singly or as couples. The relatively better-dressed ones wore trappings which appear to be fashion statements: a guy with a penis pouch that looked very much like one of those worn by a New Guinean tribesman, another had only his waist pouch and another a small haversack. The women had nothing on though one or two had the tiniest of bikinis, probably the latest in fashion to show off.

More than half of the island belongs to the French military and is out of bounds. The rest is hilly and the coastline, except for one sandy beach, is rocky. Sunworshippers have to walk down tarmac roads and when they reach the sea, step very carefully to perch, some precariously, on rocks which afford foothold or on less jagged or partially cemented spaces. Towels are then spread out beneath the shadeless sun. Many bring picnic baskets, beer, wine and plenty of water. Some come in in the morning and some after lunch and stay until 6.30 pm, before trudging uphill to their villas and hotels.

Our week climaxed with watching the Miss Ile du Levant contest over the weekend a few days later. This took place on the only sandy beach on the island and entry into the area is marked by a signpost, in French, which read, "Nudity is Obligatory".

The beach was packed; nearly every sitting and standing space was taken up by naturists with towels, mats, portable beds and beach umbrellas. As if to emphasise its innocence, there were teenagers frolicking in the sea or kayaking.

On a small, temporary platform, the male MC and his

armbanded assistants explained the rules: contestants were called by numbers 1,2,3 and as they had stepped onto the stage to loud cheers and goodnatured wolfwhistles, in some cases, they were each engaged in small chat. What is your name? What country do you come from? How long have you been here? Is this your first time?

I counted fifteen women, varying in age from nineteen to thirty-five. All white, not a single African or Asian, all nude and not the least bit self-aware. They had come from Italy, Eastern Europe, Spain and of course the home country, France. The majority, about five, came from Italy. Some paraded, some did not. There was an official photographer, who I found out later, was a shy, retired Cambridge University maths professor who comes every year.

After about an hour, the winner was picked, a French girl with an hourglass figure who seemed to be about twenty. To loud applause, as she was a popular choice, the MC announced that she would be crowned in the evening party the same night in the village square.

Reflecting on the experience of a week on the island, anticipation is the major sensation, the actual behaviour of being naked or of seeing others naked, including friends or total strangers until introduced, a secondary one. For Eve and I, we felt that once we were adjusted to seeing everyone conducting mundane activities like they were clothed, self-consciousness evaporates and no one worries. We did not become the voyeurs that we thought we might be. We were curious, yes, very curious but seeing so many in the buff and obviously enjoying themselves, satisfied our curiousity without the need for satiation. The novelty encouraged us, the very idea that we are actually doing it, for the first time, we Asians and, aiyo, from sanitary Singapore!

One cannot help the occasional sidelong look at a particularly shapely body or alluring boobs or bottoms or when someone flaunts her assets. The conformity assisted, conformity to an agreed code of behaviour. Sen related incidents of people who came to the island, went to events partially clothed and they were booed.

The climate encourages: warm, azure and absolutely crystal blue and green of the Mediterranean, the water temperature varying from 24–35°C, the sun blazing until nine in the evening, temperature between 22–24°C, everyone out for maximum tan to become universally brown. The sun became hot in the mid afternoon but broad hats helped and while the water was cool for our tropically-attuned bodies, its absolute clarity enticed. Wearing nothing was the most natural thing to do.

If the anticipated shock of Ile du Levant did not materialize, Cap d'Agde, located east of Le Levandou towards Montpellier, was a different scene. We went there straight after the week on the island, arriving on 9 August, Singapore's national day.

The Centre Rene Oltra is a sophisticated naturist campsite, with accommodation ranging from visitors who brought their own tents to structures which looked permanent, for long stayers. Families, couples and singles come to this Plage Naturiste or Naturist Beach, reached from the camp in a short walk to the water's edge.

Entry and exit are very tightly regulated: a barrier with security guards prevents unauthorized public entry and every registered camper is given a wristlet which must be worn at all times. Cars are parked outside the campsite if they arrive after 10 pm. The management is very professional.

Once settled in, our routine became familiar: morning, around 7.30 am, we would walk to St Martin's Pier and tuck into five oysters and a glass of white wine for five euros, followed by breakfast, followed by a swim if the mood took us, or a tour of the scenic places around the Centre.

Late afternoons, after 5.30 pm, on the beach is where the action takes place. We would walk past the family section of the beach, imperceptibly, into the adult section, find a crowded area and sit down on our towels. Hundreds of people were already there, a few swimming, the majority lying on towels, standing or walking, on the wide, flat, brown beach; about fifty metres inland were the white sand dunes. Suddenly, there was a commotion and many on the beach scampered quickly and made for the source of it. A crowd formed around a couple making love openly. Kissing, stroking, he entered her and pumped, she reciprocated. The people around watched, amazement showing not on their faces but in the erections of men unable to control the visual stimulation before them. Some stroked their tools. When the couple disengaged, and he stood up, a ring was visible around his private parts. The spectators began to disperse and among the men some dicks had began to dangle after the excitement. Another performance would take place in a different part of the beach.

There were regular sideshows which attract little or no attention. Returning to our towels, Sen and I saw an elderly black couple relaxing in their own way. He sat in a deck chair looking out towards the beach while next to him, the woman, bespectacled, was masturbating a young white guy without apparent enthusiasm; but he showed obvious pleasure as her left hand went up and down. All around, except for a few people actually looking, no one seemed to care. There wasn't even the air of studied nonchalance.

A flurry of movement lead to another scene. A relatively large crowd had formed around four young women who were crouched on their backs, bum to bum, such that they formed a sort of unstable table. On this moving table, a few young men were playing cards, shuffling and throwing and talking while the women tossed or pulled back their hairs and showed evident enjoyment in this innocuous game. There were good-humoured shouts, people placing bets and laughter.

Not so innocent was what we saw the next day. When we reached the scene, it was full house. We had to bend to look between spaces and legs. Serial frenching was at work; we made out about fifteen to sixteen men of various age lined up erect and this fortyish-looking woman, on her knees, licked the whole lot of them, one after the other. Some came; and while she was at it, a few males attempted to enter her from behind. At the end of this sexercise, she was obviously exhausted and had to be helped to the sea where she washed her sodden mouth and herself.

Seeing was disbelieving. Straight out of a blue flick. Naturism had become exhibitionistic and extreme, indulged for the sake of shocking, deployed as deliberate performance for a non-paying audience that cannot have enough of what they have experienced or will experience.

The niteclub scene in the port area was exotic and kinky. Nude and seminude dancing and wriggling by white, black and Latino women were watched by a similarly mixed crowd of mostly young singles and couples, some of whom were well-tattooed. Women were dressed largely in black in the most fashionable and flaunting modes. Numerous well-lit shops sold all kinds of sex enhancers and metal implements like rings for penises, nipples and navels as well as smaller rings and pins for vaginas. Some were decorative, others functional: one shop stood out for its prominently explicit photo of a vulva stretched by pins and rings. Here was another case of stretching belief. I snapped it in my digital camera to prove to disbelievers.

Pornography needs an audience to motor the stimulus-response mechanism and I must admit that, insofar as I am a member of an audience, I am guilty of incitement. How different is this from seeing a tiger show in Patpong in Bangkok? We indulge our vicarious desire to to see openly what should stay closed. We encourage by our presence.

Open and closed. Open inasmuch as there are other people sharing in the act of visual intoxication; closed, because we were expected to acknowledge that this was a distinct environment, for the campsters and those who accept the codes of behaviour of performers and audience, and was not widely known.

The only social sanction is that the laws of the country or province allow these activities in a designated place; within, even something as explicit as the serial frenching described earlier, sexual freedom of this variety abounds. Everyone knows his/her place, as performer or member of the audience, in observance of unspoken rules. We are all complicit in permitted pornography, in sanctioned sex, except that we do not perform but watch others do it—from the safety of distance.

A Perfect Exit

Aaron Ang

If you could, would you choose the way you were going to die? What would it be? More importantly, would you use it when the time was right?

These were questions Koh Kwan How and his friends often tossed around when he was much younger. Now almost all those friends were gone, and Kwan How was looking at joining them soon. At eighty-three, he had seen a lot of life and too much of death. And now he knew, very much so, which way he would choose. And yes, he was ready to use it. He knew what constituted the perfect exit. And he also knew that it was just about the right time.

All his pleasures were being snatched from him: old friends, loved ones, places he had known and loved. And now even simple, everyday pleasures were being stripped away. It seemed every time he went to his doctor, the man had another list of things he had to deny himself. Kwan How had begun calling the man Dr No: no spicy food, no Kopi-O, no alcohol, no pets … no, no, no. And, of course, no major physical exertion. His heart was far too weak, his doctor warned, just couldn't take sudden exertion. "No sex, of course," the pompous shit had instructed him. Then he had the gall to add, with that smug grin men like him seemed to take pleasure in, "But I guess in your case, that hasn't been any real temptation for a long time, has it, Mr Koh?"

That ass! Koh was tempted almost every day, at least twenty times. Just because he could no longer act on it ... Until about ten years ago, maybe less, he would make his way to Geylang once every fortnight. He'd look around, see what was on offer, then head off to a massage parlour or take a hotel room with one of the pretty China girls who trawled the coffee shops there, looking for old men like him with their plump pensions. What mainly transpired with these girls, at either the parlours or in the hotels, was what Koh and his friends used to call "a quick, helpful handshake below the waist." Well, he was an old man, even then.

But he still yearned, achingly, to make love to lovely young women as he had many years before, when he himself was much closer to their age. But that, he knew, was just the faint buzz of a dream he could never act upon. Or so he thought.

He met her through the Internet. A nephew had shown him how to connect with the contact groups; after several rounds of exploring, Kwan How came upon the kinkier groups himself. And with that, the one he wanted: the Beyond the Borders group.

He was quite surprised that so many women replied to his blunt request: "Older gentleman seeks lovely young lady to help him kill himself through sex." He was worried that at least half of them were police agents who might see this endeavour as a form of assisted suicide. But for Kwan How, it was simply a matter of "imposing a natural death"; as Dr No took delight in reminding him, vigorous sex would almost surely be the end of him. Which was exactly what he wanted. It was, for Koh, the perfect exit.

And this one was perfect in her own way. He had scanned through at least a dozen photos sent to him on the Net, and they all looked interesting, but he was jolted when her picture came up. Su Lon. No, it wasn't her, couldn't be; but it looked so much like her, as he remembered her, from over sixty years earlier.

Su Lon was the first love of his life. In some ways, still the only special love. His first love, his first sexual experience. And now this one—what was that name? Sharlayne, this Sharlayne looked so much like his Su Lon. As if she had somehow sprung over all those decades, as lovely as ever, preserved simply by his memory of her. Incredible.

He made contact and they bounced several e-mails back and forth before he sent her his telephone number. Then there was nothing for four days. He began to think she was just playing with him, using him as a joke she could share with her gleefully callous friends. But late that Sunday evening the phone rang, waking him up. "Mr Koh, this is Sharlayne. From that Beyond the Borders group? You wanted me to help you with your project?"

"Yes, yes," he replied. "That's right. I ... I would like your help. Very much."

They arranged to meet the following weekend, at his place. He would take care of all the formalities, he assured her, including any necessary legal precautions. There would be no way any authorities would associate her with his death. This would be seen as purely a consensual act between two adults— with very unfortunate consequences. He was surprised that she didn't seem too concerned about this part of the arrangement though.

When she arrived around 4 pm Saturday, he was waiting nervously for her. In fact, Koh was perched on a metal chair facing the front door, reading fitfully from a newspaper while throwing glances at the open door. He had almost convinced himself that she wasn't going to come after all. *Fool, why would such a lovely young woman want to do something as perverse as this anyway? With someone like you?*

When the bell rang, he couldn't see her through the grill: evidently, she was standing off to the side. Koh quickly threw his paper down, hauled himself up, went to let her in. When he opened the grill, she peeked from around the corner. "Mr Koh, is it?"

"Yes, yes," Koh replied. "Koh Kwan How. Just Kwan, if you like. Kwan is fine."

She nodded and stepped in. She seemed strangely shy at this point, considering how they had met and what she was there for. She was even looking down, demure in a way he would never have expected from this new, anything-goes generation. When she glanced up, this girl looked even more like Su Lon than she had on the monitor. He was staring at her, transfixed, until finally she peered at him nervously. "What?"

"Incredible," Koh said in a raspy voice. "Oh, sorry, it's

just ... You look very much like someone I ... I knew. A long, long time ago."

"Do I? Oh yeah, thanks. You look like a lot of people I know too, uncle." Koh winced at her calling him uncle, but not enough for her to notice.

He offered her a drink, then found her a can of the Yeo's chrysanthemum tea she had asked for. After taking a long draught, she frowned and looked around the room, as if assessing his taste in furnishings or sense of feng shui. For a moment, he was even afraid that she was about to tell him that she had reconsidered and now just wanted to call the whole thing off. But instead, she said something that stunned him. "You want to, like, take our clothes off, uncle, see what we're talking about?"

"Yes, yes, that might be ... That's a good way to start, I'm sure." He was still a little stunned by her directness when she started to pull off her shirt, then removed her pants. As she stood there in only bra and panties, he mechanically put his hands to his shirt and began fumbling with the buttons, still staring at her, enthralled.

Curiously, she removed her panties first, then thrust her hips forward slightly, as if displaying some unusual wares to a prospective buyer. He was still fumbling with that same top button as she reached back, unhooked her bra and let it drop to the floor. Koh's fingers froze on the button. *Dear God, even her body looks like Su Lon's.* Or at least the way he remembered it. The compact, tight breasts, the neat, dark triangle of pubic hair with the delicate slit in the middle—everything, so close to how he remembered it. He reacted immediately. It was ... he didn't

249

want to think how many years since he was able to even get this hard without considerable manual or oral stimulation.

"You ... you have a fantastic body," he gasped.

"My tits are too small," she replied, looking down as if to test his evaluation. "My friends keep telling me I should go and get them enlarged. It doesn't cost that much at this one place I heard about."

"Oh no. Oh no, no, don't ... don't do that. They're incredible. They fit your body perfectly. You couldn't ask for a better pair of breasts than what you've got there."

"Well, they'll do for now, I guess," she concluded, giving a soft shrug. He had just managed to get the first button undone at that point and was trying to concentrate intensely on the rest of the task when she stepped forward. "Here, let me help you with that," she said.

Again, he was taken aback as she reached those delicate hands—so like Su Lon's—out to touch him. His fingers were frozen again, and she had to move his hands away gently, then she slowly undid every button. He stared at her now deeply intent face, not wanting to peer at his own body. He was deeply ashamed of it, even repulsed at its wattles of loose flesh, its liver flecks splashed sporadically all over his torso and arms, its wrinkles even in what he once thought unlikely places.

After removing the shirt, she reached down and unbuckled his belt, opened the trousers and eased them down over his hips. When they sagged around his knees, he reached down and hastily pulled them off himself. Again, he was embarrassed: the elaborate webbing of varicose veins made his legs an unpleasant sight, especially to himself.

But again, she was being generous, or just polite. She ignored the varicose legs and began staring directly at the sharp rise in his shorts. She looked at him, smiled, nudged the near-erection slightly up and forwards, then pulled down the briefs.

"Oh look, you're almost ready for action, isn't it?"

"I didn't intend to make your trip over here wasted, la. Bedroom's over this way."

He pointed to the room at the end of a hallway, and guided her towards it. Along the way, he grabbed a towel off a nearby chair and drooped it in front of his crotch. He felt giddy with this wholly new experience, but still couldn't help feeling funny walking around naked in his own flat, especially with a young woman present.

As they headed towards the bedroom, Koh suddenly stopped near the bulky Peranakan table standing guard in the middle of the room and pointed to a small leather bag perched near the edge. "Those are for you by the way. Don't forget to take them when you leave."

"What is it?

"It's ... I know we said no money, no payment, but it's presents. Some presents I got for you. Just thought it will be nice, lah. The money won't do me any more good anyway, will it?"

Before he could say anything else, she'd darted over to the table and started fumbling through the bag. "Hey, those are surprises, lah. For later. Afterwards."

"Can't I open one, just one? That's all."

Even her little-girl manner when she asked reminded him of

Su Lon. He smiled back at her. "Alright, just one." He raised an admonishing finger. "But no more!"

She smiled and chose something in a long, narrow box. "Ooo, what's this one? Something we might be able to use in there? Looks like it."

He chortled. "No, it's just for you. It's all things I thought you might like."

She slid the top off the thin box, reached in and pulled out a slender gold necklace. "Oh, that's beautiful," she whispered. "It's ... wow, just so sweet of you." Koh smiled sheepishly. She stepped over and gave him a warm kiss, one that actually tasted of mild affection. He was embarrassed—and very pleased. She then broke into a wide smile. "Can I put it on now? Right now?"

"Now?? But I thought we're going to—"

"Oh, please, Mr Koh! I want to have something like this to wear. I'm always a little shy when I'm totally naked with some guy for the first time." She then cast a quick, playful glance down at his towel.

This made him laugh again, after which he nodded and watched as she placed the necklace against her smooth throat. She then turned, holding the ends behind and just off her neck, inviting him to latch it. Which he did, with care and some affection. She rushed over to the smeared mirror a few feet away and observed herself, making funny faces, as if she were suddenly the only person in the room. Koh himself admired her naked back, the nicely framed shoulders. "This is just so nice. So sweet." She turned with a deeply set smile, and Kwan How suddenly felt as close to her as he had to any woman, any person, in a long time. It was good that it should all end like this. This was becoming more and more perfect.

When they reached the bedroom, she jumped onto the bed as if she needed to try it out first. She pounded it with her fists, then started kicking her legs up and down. Koh was standing just inside the doorway, the towel still dangling over his private parts. "Suitable?" he asked, his eyes slowly surveying the arch of her back, the slopes of her buttocks, her nicely formed legs and feet.

"Very suitable," she replied.

She then rolled over on her back, propped her head up on the three pillows and spread her legs. "Going to join me, Mr Koh? It's nice down here. *Very* nice." As she said those last two words, she started stroking herself, at the same time slipping her tongue out and gliding it slowly over her lips.

Koh laughed again; she looked so much like Su Lon, but was so different in her behaviour. She was—what was that word he liked?—frisky. Yes, *so* frisky. Su Lon had been *so* wonderfully shy, right up until the moment he first entered her. Of course, that was expected of girls, especially Chinese girls, in those days.

But part of Su Lon's reluctance with Kwan How stemmed from the fact that she was engaged to another man at the time. Oh, there was nothing like love there—on either side apparently—but it was a good match in most other ways. The war and the Japanese occupation had stranded that fiancé in Ceylon. Meanwhile, Kwan How's position at the docks enabled him to get his hands on extra goods: contraband rice, salted fish and cooking oil—some of which he gave to Su Lon's family. That's how they started to get close. And then there was that keen natural attraction that happens between two young, good-looking people.

Had there been no war, Su Lon would have surely remained a traditional Chinese woman, going to her wedding bed a virgin, with a man she barely knew and had no great affection for. That was the deal back then: sex as duty, marriage as transaction, love as a possible bonus—but only later.

Except that she and Kwan How found themselves more and more drawn to each other. Besides, Su Lon didn't know if she would ever see this fiancé again; it was all up to fate whether any of them would survive that war and the occupation. Which is why she and Kwan How became lovers, their daily flirts with arrest and death only intensifying the passion and tonic release of their couplings. Yes, being so close to death, Kwan How had lived more intensely than he would ever again in his life.

Everything could have been different, should have been different. But the war ended, Su Lon's betrothed returned, they married, and Kwan How saw or heard very little of her for the next year and a half. Until he got that note from her brother. Sweet, delicate Su Lon, who had survived the storm of perils thrown up by the Japanese occupation, stepped in front of a Bentley driven by some *blur* Dutch woman. She was dead by the time they got her to a hospital. Publicly, everyone said it was an accident, but under the soothing drone of officialese, there was a swarm of dark rumours.

"Is everything alright?" Sharlayne called from the bed.

Koh looked up at her and nodded. Yes, everything was alright; maybe that was the perfect exit Su Lon had chosen for herself. "She heard another music," was the cryptic way a friend once described the way she died. And now Koh was there, at the edge of grasping an amazing dream for his own departure. *Perhaps this was what she'd meant by another music?*

Sharlayne was now stroking herself more energetically, three fingers working deeply into the gash, moving about in slow, circular turns. "Everything is wonderful," Koh finally said, "more wonderful than I could have imagined it."

"Well, why don't you come over here, uncle, and we'll see how we can make it even better." Koh nodded in agreement and strode over, dropping the towel only as he made his way onto the bed.

He had become soft by now and only when he put his legs and side against her flesh did he again feel the stirrings in his loins and in his chest which had been so strong just minutes before. He wanted to get hard as quickly as he could, to couple with this young woman. Wanted to return, however briefly, to feeling life intensely. His look obviously conveyed this, as Sharlayne asked if he wanted some help. Suddenly feeling humiliated, Koh simply nodded. "Yeah?" she said sympathetically. Koh then leaned over and whispered in her ear.

But she said she didn't want to go down on him, claiming she "wasn't into" oral sex. He didn't believe her, of course. But she was solicitous: to get him harder, she began stroking his cock, then licked her fingers lavishly, moistening his member as she stroked it a second time. She then stuck two fingers up her vagina, pulled them out and rubbed the warm juice along the high bend of his cock.

Koh could not even remember the last time he had been this hard, decades certainly. He wanted desperately to get inside her and rasp this out. But at that moment, there was an abrupt change in her demeanour: she rose and knelt on the bed. For the first time since they had started undressing, she looked grim. "Are you sure this can really kill you?" she asked, "Really?"

"That's what my doctor keeps saying." She nodded, but did not look very convinced.

"You ever asked for a second opinion?"

He smiled sheepishly. "I'm about to get one." She frowned again, concern darkening her delicate features. She cast her eyes down and started tracing some arcane pattern in the sheets with one finger. "Look, it's what I really want, okay?" he assured her. "I have no doubts about this." She glanced up at him, cautiously, from the corner of her eye. He was afraid he might lose this right here, so close to what he wanted. "Are you going to deny a nice old man his last request?"

"No," she answered after a short pause. "It's something I really want to try myself." She then leaned over, gave him a light kiss on the forehead, and pressing her head against his neck, hugged him awkwardly. This was good enough; at this stage in his life, the "uncle" had sharply pared down what he expected from perfect.

Koh now smiled, a little sadly, at her. Sharlayne took this as a cue, lay back flat on the bed and stared straight up, as if studying something on the ceiling. Koh kept smiling; it didn't matter, not now. She spread her legs, her thin legs, and Koh thought he would begin by putting his legs tightly against hers and then massaging the insides of her thighs—as he had done that first time with Su Lon.

But as he tried to splay his legs that far, he found that his weak knees weren't up to the task. He fell forward, giving out a yelp of pain.

Sharlayne, who had continued peering up at the ceiling until then, swung around swiftly, asked if Koh was alright, and rubbed his shoulders in consolation. He tried to shake it off as lightly as he could. "Guess one shouldn't try new tricks, wah," he said with a feeble laugh. The embarrassment actually hurt more than the physical pain. She asked if he wanted her to get on top, but he mumbled that he preferred being on top of her. She nodded, then lay back on the bed, her hair draped capriciously across the pillows.

Still smarting a little from his fall, Koh now crawled up to Sharlayne gingerly. When he was positioned just right, he breathed deeply, then carefully arched his groin above hers. Sharlayne reached up, took his cock and slowly started to pull him into her. *Oh wei!* She felt fantastic, not like some human masturbation device—like those Geylang whores—but like a woman, just the way Su Lon once was with him. He slowly started thrusting his cock into her, getting the feel of her vagina.

He then began pumping harder, harder, first just with his butt and hips, then with his upper body as well. He was giving her everything he could, trying to fuck her in a way that she

257

would always remember, fucking as if there were no tomorrow.

Because that was the whole point, wasn't it? There shouldn't be any tomorrow for Koh Kwan How. This was his perfect exit, this act of lovemaking as fantastic as his very first one with Su Lon, with a girl who looked so much like Su Lon did back then.

As he began thrusting himself fearsomely into her, Sharlayne herself seemed to become more and more excited. Her eyes were shut tight, which should have disturbed Koh, but it didn't. If that made her feel better with him, even if she was thinking about some boyfriend or pop star, then it was the right thing. He started fucking even more furiously, giving everything he could draw up. His body's frantic stabs seemed to be moving a beat or two ahead of his breaths and he was starting to get giddy. Was this it then, was this how it would all end? He tried speeding up even more, pushing himself harder, more urgently.

It was then that Sharlayne finally opened her eyes, focused point blank into his so all she could see were his eyes seeing hers and, clutching him desperately by the lower lean of his back, she moaned, "Oh God, fuck me, fuck me hard, *fuck me this way forever!*"

As he responded to her, his words came out in erratic gasps, pulled out from what reserve wind he wasn't using for the fucking. "Yes ... yes, I'll ... as ... hard ... as ... you ... need. As ... hard ... as. ..." He was unable to force out any more words.

Without opening her eyes, she moaned, "Yes, do it, do it—deeper, more deeper. Oh please—all the way."

Koh plunged as deep as he could into her, pumping with everything he had left in him. His eyes, too, were closed tightly now, yet he saw her face as clearly as he had just a few moments before. "Oh yes, dee … deeper. Here you are, finally—my angel. My lovely, lovely angel of death."

And just as he said it, he burst, his cock pulsating in a sad stutter of throbs. His semen came out in short, painful jerks. He started giving short cries as he came; he realised he must sound like a wounded seal thrown onto a beach. He was fighting to snatch random breaths, his lungs and throat felt seared, his nostrils stung, every part of his body was starting to rebel as pain coursed through him from neck to ankles.

All of which, he realised, meant that he was still alive. His perfect plan had failed.

He felt the need to explain, to apologise, to share one more thing more with this lovely young woman. "I didn't think I'd … still be able to … " He stopped, and realised he was crying. After several moments, he forced himself to shut off the tears, then he turned back to explain.

As he did, he realised that she had said nothing since his climax; in fact, she had barely budged. As he finally looked at her, it was as if a huge slap was there just waiting for him to turn around: Sharlayne seemed to be unconscious, eyes closed. Not only that, her breathing was extremely shallow, like that of some people he had seen just before they left.

With all the fretted strength he could muster, he pulled himself up and tried shaking her. At this, her eyes opened slightly and one hand moved weakly to the necklace. She raised it slightly, said, "Thank you again. Very generous," before her eyelids slid closed once more. This time, she seemed to be hardly breathing at all.

Koh struggled from the bed and made his way to the table where the phone rested. Hands shaking so badly he was barely up to the task, he punched out the number of his one close nephew, Daniel. He had arranged for Daniel to drop by at six, to "pick something up." Of course, he was supposed to find Koh dead. But that was well over an hour away. Koh needed him there *now*.

He cursed when the droning buzzes ended with the recorded voice saying, "Sorry, the M1 customer you just called is not responding. Please try again later." The old man slammed his phone back into its cradle. *Stupid, so stupid! Why even have a handphone if you're not going to leave it on, make yourself available when people need you in an emergency like this?*

So, Koh reluctantly called emergency services. And after hanging up, he settled himself into the creaking chair next to the table and stared over at her, his quivering hands set flat on his thighs. *Oh my God, this is how I sit at a wake. But that's not the situation here; she's young, she'll be fine, this is most likely just … just what?*

Yes, just what was this anyway? For that matter, why had this lovely young woman agreed to come over and have sex with some pathetic old man who had some crazy plan to end his own life? He was well acquainted with his own plan, how beautiful it was, but he suddenly wondered what her reason was for participating. As the heavy moments dragged past, these questions grew more and more vexing for Kwan How.

He pulled himself up, staggered over and stood at the foot

of the bed. Her mouth now hung open; she didn't seem to be breathing at all. Koh wanted to put his hand to the mouth to test her for breaths, maybe try to feel a pulse. But at the moment he was terrified to come any closer. He stared, fixed in a state just short of shock. *How did this girl end up like this in my bed?* Just lying there, maybe dead, she looked—he hated to even visit this thought—but she looked … yes, perfect.

He picked up a blanket from the edge of the bed and spread it over her, to protect her decency for when the medical-emergency team arrived. And he still could not keep from staring at her. She had this amazing look etched into her face. As if she had just achieved something beautiful. And now he imagined that that mouth was open so that she could sing some sublime, silent song. Yes, there was now something irredeemably perfect about this moment. Although it was mainly hers, he had a share of it.

Koh dropped the towel wrapped around his own midriff and climbed onto the bed. He lifted the blanket and started to slide under it. But no, although he ached to touch her naked body again with his, he realised he couldn't.

He wrapped the blanket tightly all around her, pulled up closer and folded his arm around her. She still felt so warm, looked so lovely here. He rested his head firmly against hers, listening as hard as he could.

At first, he just wanted to hear some breathing, but when he couldn't detect any, he strained his ears to listen to that silent song he imagined her singing. *This was surely the anthem of the perfect exit.* When he, too, could hear it, he would know how to reach that point, as she did. He waited.

Acknowledgements

We would be remiss if we didn't acknowledge certain organisations and individuals who contributed to the making of this ground-breaking anthology.

To Quarterly Literary Review of Singapore and Singapore Writers Guild for helping spread the word throughout the local writing community.

To Writers Connect, the writers' workshop and support arm of Word Forward, both for alerting all writers in its influential sphere to the project and especially for workshopping several stories written for this collection.

To Pipi Lee, for patience that goes beyond any standard definition of patience; and to Pam, for listening, and talking about sex into the wee hours of the morning.

THE GOOD GIRL by Alice Lee Am©2006, Alice Lee Am. CLEAN SEX by Ricky Low©2006, Ricky Low. DANCER FROM THE DANCE by Felix Cheong©2003, Felix Cheong. First published in *Broken by the Rain* (Firstfruits), 2003. Reprinted by permission of the author. NIGHT AT PASSION TOUCH by Hari Kumar©2006, Hari Kumar. Excerpted from the novel *Killing the Red God*. ON THE SOFA by Kirpal Singh©2005, Kirpal Singh. TWO MEN AND A PLAN by O Thiam Chin©2006, O Thiam Chin. AND THEN SHE CAME by Jonathan Lim©2006,

BEST OF SOUTHEAST ASIAN EROTICA

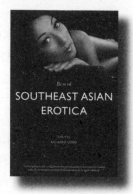

Richard Lord (Editor)

The *Best of Southeast Asian Erotica* includes fiction written by leading writers in Thailand, Malaysia, Indonesia and the Philippines, as well as from Singapore. In "The Sex Thing with the Tempoyak", a couple in their first year of marriage pull themselves out of burgeoning bedroom boredom when they discover the joys of an ancient Javanese sex manual; in "Awakening", a young Malaysian girl gets her hands on an anthology called *Best of Southeast Asian Erotica* that her parents have hidden for years and starts to learn about sensuality and its hidden treasures.

Writers in this anthology include renowned Malaysian filmmaker Amir Muhammad, Yusuf Martin, Ricky Low, Jim Algie, Brenton Rossow and John Burdett, author of *Bangkok 8* and *Bangkok Tattoo*.

ISBN: 978-981-08-5436-2
(www.monsoonbooks.com.sg/bookpage_0854362.html)